MW01043351

MILE HIGH

A NOVEL BY

MICHAEL ALEXANDER

Protea Publishing

Copyright (c)2004 The Author. All rights reserved.

This is a work of fiction.

First Edition

ISBN 1-59344- 061-8   soft cover

ISBN 1-59344- 062-6   hard cover

USA Library Of Congress Control Number: 2004107652

Protea Publishing (Imprint)
Las Vegas, Nevada, USA
southsky@earthlink.net
www.proteapublishing.com

"There is something in the unselfish and self-sacrificing love of a brute, which goes directly to the heart of him who has had frequent occasion to test the paltry friendship and gossamer fidelity of mere MAN."

Edgar Allan Poe

"When man is driven by fear, he'd better have on all season radials."

Anonymous by request

October 21st, 1990

The tires of the old car screeched to a halt. David Lemming looked up at the old house through his windshield. There was just enough twilight for him to see. The old house was separated into a duplex, and it was a two story one. The police were already there.

He got out and walked to the front door. A couple of armed men stood in his way, but he flashed an id. It seemed to ease them, and they let him through. The sense of dread was creeping into him. He walked in and immediately sized up the situation. Inspector Hal Bradford was at the top of the flight of winding stairs. Seeing him, the inspector waved his hand.

"Come on up, Mr. Lemming. I was expecting you to show up sooner or later."

Lemming strode up the stairs quickly. He flashed the inspector a smile. He did not care much for the old man, but was always respectful. The man had some clout in the Denver metropolitan area.

"The Body's in the second bedroom," the inspector said. "I'll warn you, it's not pretty."

Lemming nodded and stepped into the room. He took in the sight and let out a low whistle. On a four-poster queen bed lay a woman, possibly in her mid twenties. There was a large serrated knife plunged into her throat. She had very little clothes on. There were two men taking pictures, and a policeman taking notes. He turned back to the inspector and grimaced.

"You're right, it's not pretty at all."

Inspector Bradford set his jaw. His clean-shaven face held a look of disgust. "It was probably her fiancé. A guy named Joe Thurman. I'm having Masters pick him up."

"You're going to question him? Have any leads?"

"Don't you know, Mr. Lemming? In about 75 percent of all murder cases the murderer is usually a husband, wife, boyfriend, or girlfriend."

5

Lemming ignored the obvious shot. "I'm in on the questioning," he stated.

Bradford rolled his eyes. "What, another notch on your bedpost of murder cases? Let's just leave this one to us, buddy. This looks like a clear cut case of..."

"Not a chance," interrupted Lemming. "You want the case solved? I'm your man and you know it."

Yeah, you're the man all right, thought the inspector. Harvard educated, top of his class, and generally thought of as the top private investigator in Denver. It's too bad you're such an asshole.

"We don't have many clues," he said aloud.

Lemming kicked a broken light bulb that lay beside the bed of the dead woman. "She did put up a struggle, didn't she? Broken shit all over the place, clothes torn apart..."

"Wouldn't you?"

"I guess so," Lemming said, smiling. He picked up the inspector's notes from the table. "Let's see...dead girl's name is Virginia Kelly. She is... I'm sorry; she was a grad student at U.C. Boulder. Her major was psychology with a concentration in abnormal psych. Parents named Brad and Margaret, living in San Antonio. You seem to have covered all the bases."

The inspector smiled dryly. "You know what they say. Leave no stone unturned."

"I said seemed to have covered all the bases. Often, things are not as they seem."

The inspector coughed. "Really?"

Lemming put the notes back down. "How old was she? Who found the body? How many hours has she been dead? Any motives? Any clues? Are drugs involved? This is a young woman, inspector!"

The inspector did not seem bothered. "She's twenty four, in the prime of life. Her roommate found her. We don't know how many hours she's been dead yet, nor do we know of anyone with a motive. We have few clues. Drugs are always a possibility. Lastly, this is quite a tragedy...she was twenty four."

"Yes, quite tragic," Lemming said in a bored voice. "Who's the roommate?"

A couple of doctors walked into the room and went over to

the body. The inspector looked at them carefully. "Roommate's name is Amy something. She went out with her boyfriend to dinner. She got back to find this. There's another roommate named Colleen something, but she's not been here all day."

Lemming bit his lower lip. "So you don't think this Amy something had anything to do with it?"

"No I do not," the inspector said flatly. He looked at his watch. "I'm getting out of here. You going to hang around?"

"Yeah, I want to ask these doctors some questions."

"Suit yourself," inspector Bradford said and walked out of the room. Most of the people had left already, except for the two doctors and a couple of reporters who were still taking photographs of the scene. Lemming looked at the dead girl again. He then looked at his watch. It was 10:30 p.m. He had walked into the house thirty minutes ago. He wished he was partying with Lisa, but business before pleasure had always been his motto. He did not get where he was by being complacent. Besides, this was imperative. He was so engrossed in his thoughts, that he did not notice the tall, dark haired man that was now standing beside him.

"Hi, you must be the guy in charge here!"

Lemming came to with a jump. "Uh, who are you?"

"I'm the dead girl's...I'm Virginia's cousin. My name's John Kirby."

Lemming stared at him for a second. "Mr. Kirby, who let you in?"

"The cop downstairs was very nice when I told him who I was."

"Oh he was nice was he?" Lemming said, disgusted. "Security sucks around this place."

"Look, Mr.."

"Lemming. David Lemming"

"Mr. Lemming, I assure you that I am just here to help identify my cousin."

Lemming smiled. He looked at the doctors, both of whom were still tending to the body. "Let's step out in the hall, Mr. Kirby."

Kirby obliged. Once out in the hall, Lemming looked straight at him, his smile still on his face. "Mr. Kirby, how do you know your cousin is dead? The story hasn't had time to hit the air

7

yet."

Kirby's facial expression changed to one of confusion. He thought for a minute and said, "I heard it on the police scanner. I was close by, so I had to come."

"I see…" Lemming said slowly.

"I can't believe someone would want to kill Virginia. She didn't have any enemies. She was a sweet girl. What possible reason..."

Lemming interrupted the taller man with a wave of his hand. "It may have been a simple case of rape and murder."

"Rape? You think so? How do you..."

"How do I know? When a girl is found spread eagle naked on a bed murdered, that's usually the case," Lemming said, stretching the truth a little. He wanted to watch the man's reactions very carefully.

"My God!" Kirby was horrified.

Lemming took another good look at John Kirby. He made up his mind that he was there for another reason.

"Mr. Kirby, do you know her fiancé?"

"Who, Joe? I know of him, never met."

"How long has he been engaged to her?"

"I think a year and a half."

Lemming's eyebrows shot up. "A year and a half? And you've never met the guy?"

"Well, I don't live here. I live in Boulder. I go to school at Colorado."

"So was she."

Kirby nodded. Lemming led him to the door. "You really don't have to identify the body now, Mr. Kirby. Just go home, and don't leave town. Later, the police will call you, I'm sure!"

Kirby got upset. He stepped outside, protesting. "I really think I can help you tonight, Chief Lemming."

Lemming laughed. "Detective Lemming. Just go home tonight, bud. Mind if I walk you to your car?"

As Kirby got in his late model Ford, Lemming took a quick peek inside the car. He saw what he thought he would see.

"Looks like someone stole your CB radio, Mr. Kirby." he said, smiling.

"I better go," Kirby said nervously and drove off. Lemming

stared after him for a while and then went back into the house. The doctors were just finishing up. One of them looked up at Lemming as he walked in. The dead body was now wrapped up and being carted away. Lemming extended his hand to the doctor.

"Hello doctor, I'm..."

"David Lemming, P.I.," the doctor finished for him. "You're more well known than you think."

Lemming smiled and shook his hand. "My reputation precedes me. Hope all you've heard is good."

"Mostly," the doctor said. "I'm Dr. Sheppard. Geoff Sheppard. This is some nasty business, huh?"

"I'm used to it. What was the time of death?"

"I'd say between 5:00 and 6:30 this evening. The autopsy will tell us more."

"Was she raped?"

"I'm not sure. There certainly was a struggle, but no trace of penetration or semen. Of course that doesn't mean she wasn't raped. We'll find out more tomorrow."

"Have a good day, doctor," Lemming said, getting ready to leave. "I'm sure I'll see you again."

As he left the house, Lemming decided that he would visit Inspector Hal Bradford in his office tomorrow. Right now, he had to find Lisa. A smile found his face as he drove off.

October 22nd, 1990

Inspector Bradford picked up the ringing telephone in his office.

"Hello, Bradford speaking."

"Inspector. David Lemming's here to see you."

Bradford looked at his watch. 8:25 a.m. Lemming was an early riser.

"Send him in"

The door opened and David Lemming walked in. He was unshaven, and his hair was a mess. Bradford smiled.

"Rough night? You look like shit."

"Thank you," Lemming said, noisily sitting down. "However, I didn't come here to discuss my resemblance to human waste."

Bradford's face got serious. "No word from the autopsy yet, if that's why you're here. I do have Joe Thurman coming in for questioning."

"Good. I'll be there to lend you a hand," Lemming declared.

"Can I stop you?"

"No."

The phone rang again. Bradford hit the speakerphone button.

"Yes?"

"Inspector, he's ready."

"Right on time," Bradford said, getting up. "Come on, let's go."

They walked down a flight of steps and turned into a hallway. The second door to the right was marked "INTERVIEW ROOM".

"He's in there," Bradford said. "Let me and Davis do the talking, ok?"

Lemming held up his hands in mock protest. "I won't say a word!"

They walked in. Detective Chandler Davis, a small dark

haired man, was sitting across a very nervous looking man wearing glasses. He looked to be in his early thirties. They both looked up at them as they entered. Detective Davis acknowledged Lemming's presence with a smile. The two had met before.

"Ok, let's get down to business," Bradford said, pulling up a chair. "You are Joe Thurman?"

The man nodded. Lemming did not sit down. Instead, he leaned up against the wall and watched.

"Mr. Thurman, you are acquainted with a Miss Virginia Kelly?"

"Yes sir, she was my fiancé."

"You are aware that she was murdered last night?"

"Yes, I know."

Bradford eyed him carefully. "Mr. Thurman, what is your occupation?"

Thurman was surprised by the question for a second. "I'm a tooling engineer at Compro Industries."

"And what does that involve?"

"Um, project set ups, fixture design and pricing, so on..." Thurman said, his eyes narrowing. "Listen, why are you asking me these questions? Why am I here?"

"Routine questioning," Bradford said, smiling in reassurance. "Now, tell me what were you doing around say, five or six in the evening yesterday?"

Thurman settled back in his chair. "Well, let's see...I was eating supper around 5:30. I know because I ate right after my jogging route, which was over around 5:15."

"Where were you eating?"

"At my house."

Not as nervous as he looks, Bradford thought. He's answering quite calmly.

"Did you have any contact with your fiancé yesterday?"

"I called her around one o'clock. We didn't talk long."

"And how did she sound to you?"

"Okay, I guess," Thurman said, frowning. "Although she seemed a little aloof."

Bradford leaned forward. "How so?"

"Well, she sounded like she wasn't really listening to all I had to say. It was as if her mind was somewhere else."

David Lemming spoke from across the room. "What was your conversation about?"

Thurman turned around. "Um, nothing, just small talk, her studies, my work, etcetera."

Lemming smiled. "What about her? What did she do?"

Thurman seemed to get nervous. "She was a student. I thought you guys knew that."

Lemming shook his head. "No, you misunderstand. I meant, what did she do for money?"

Thurman grew increasingly nervous. "Um, she worked at a local restaurant as a waitress."

Lemming did not move from his spot beside the wall. "Mr. Thurman, did your fiancé use drugs?"

"No way!"

"Isn't it hard to support a cocaine habit on the wages of a waitress?"

"What are you talking about?" Thurman said, half screaming. He turned to Bradford. "Who the hell is he anyway?"

Lemming walked up to Thurman and grabbed his face. He stared straight into his eyes and said, "I'm just a guy who's wondering if your fiancé was a slut."

Thurman reddened. Then he leaped at Lemming, but Davis held him back. Lemming backed up, a crooked smile on his face.

"All right, Lemming, outside!" Bradford yelled, and yanked him out the door and into the hallway.

"What the hell was that?"

"Oh come on inspector, you can sit there and ask bullshit questions all day, but the fact is that Virginia Kelly was a drug addict. She slept around for money to support her drug habit. What's more, that idiot in there knows it."

"How the hell do you know this?"

"Inspector, if you had bothered to do your homework, you'd know it too," Lemming said, kicking a trashcan over. "When are you going to start a case from the ground up, and learn EVERYTHING about the victim before you get out your damn magnifying glass?"

The inspector was not happy. "Listen, I'm going to let you back in there, but your ass is out if you say one more thing."

Lemming calmed down. "Do one thing. Ask him if he

12

cheated on HER."

Bradford blinked. He was not sure how to handle this brash and arrogant man and his onion breath right under his nose. What was more frustrating was that he might actually be right...he had not done a great job investigating the case yet, but the truth was, he had not had any time. Lemming had obviously spent all night researching the victim. He relented.

"All right. I'll see what I can do."

The two went back in the room. Thurman rose up out of his seat quickly.

"Listen, I'm not talking to that guy!"

"Calm down, you won't have to. Sit down and answer this: I understand your fiancé had two roommates. Is that so?"

"Yes, two roommates and two suitemates."

"Suitemates?"

"Yeah, the house is a duplex, you know. The other two girls lived on the other side."

"So everyone in the building is female?"

"Yes."

"Who are these roommates? What do they do? We were not able to ask them too many questions, and we cannot locate one of them."

Thurman grinned. "It doesn't matter anyway. Those two are real airheads. You need to talk to the suitemates. That McKinley girl is a sharp one. She probably saw everything."

"Their names?" Bradford pressed.

"Well, her roommates were Amy and Colleen, I don't even know their last names," Thurman said. "The suitemates were Sandy Devereaux and Traci McKinley. I don't really know what any of them do, I think they are all students."

"All attend U.C. Boulder? That's a good drive isn't it?"

"Yeah, but they carpooled. Virginia always told me that she hated Boulder's social scene, so she preferred to live in Denver. A lot of people do it you know."

Bradford kept writing on his notepad. Now he looked up. "Ok, Mr. Thurman, now I am going to ask you a difficult question, so try and answer it to the best of your ability. Do you think Virginia cheated on you?"

Thurman remained calm. He seemed to be mulling things

13

over in his head. Finally he spoke.

"I can't answer that."

"Can't, or won't?"

"Both."

"Very well," Bradford said sharply, "Then answer this: Did you cheat on her?"

For the first time, a smile came across Thurman's face. It was not a nice smile.

"How do you know I won't lie to you?"

Bradford stayed silent for a moment, and then fished out a cigarette out of his pocket. He lit it carefully and got up from his chair. He strolled over to the back wall and looked straight at it.

"Mr. Thurman, you may go," he said slowly.

"Thank God!" Thurman exclaimed and got up. "It's been real, guys."

As he strode out, Bradford called after him. "Mr. Thurman, don't leave town."

"I feel like such a suspect!" Thurman said sarcastically. As he shut the door behind him, he flashed Lemming a threatening look. Lemming grinned at him as the door slammed shut.

"Guy's a damn liar," he said.

Detective Davis looked up from his chair. He had been recording the whole interview. "He was definitely hiding something."

Lemming nodded in agreement. "A real son of a bitch. Well, let's get out of here."

The trio walked back up to the inspector's office where they found a message from his secretary to call a Dr. Shockley at the morgue.

"Must be the pathologist on the case," Bradford said and dialed a number. He pressed the speakerphone button.

"City General."

"Dr. Shockley, please. This is Inspector Hal Bradford of the Denver city police returning his call."

"One moment please."

"Today's weather calls for partly cloudy skies over Denver, with a high in the mid fifties. Tonight, the mile high city will experience a low of..."

"Hello, this is Dr. Shockley."

14

"Dr. Shockley? Inspector Bradford here. Returning your call. You have some information for me?"

"Yes inspector, I do. That girl who was murdered last night, Miss Virginia Kelly?"

"Yes?"

"I did the autopsy on her this morning. It seems she was quite a drug user."

"Really," Bradford said, exchanging glances with Lemming.

"Large traces of heroin and T.H.C in her blood. Needle marks on her arm, the whole nine yards."

"How large a dose..."

"No, no, no, not large enough to kill her. The knife killed her all right."

"I see. Anything else?"

"Yes. I am pretty sure she was unconscious when she received her fatal knife wound. The large bump on her head leads me to believe that someone hit her while her back was turned."

Inspector Bradford frowned. He had not expected this. He leaned in closer to the speaker.

"Dr. Shockley, that is very unexpected. Do you think it was someone she knew?"

"Well, I'm not a detective, inspector, but it would seem so."

David Lemming spoke up. "Dr. Shockley, this is David Lemming. I'm an investigator with an interest in the case. Tell me, was the victim raped?"

"Raped?" Shockley said, laughing, "I just told you she was knocked unconscious!"

"She could still be raped."

Shockley's voice got grave as he realized the meaning of this statement. He cleared his throat and said, "No, she was not raped."

"You are sure?" Lemming pressed on.

"Absolutely."

"Thank you Dr. Shockley, please call me back if anything else develops," Bradford cut in and hung up. He looked at Lemming disgustedly.

"What is it with you and this rape thing anyway?" he asked, gesturing with his hands wildly.

"Why strip her down? Why fake the signs of a struggle and break lamps and furniture if she was unconscious? To make it look like rape? And yet, if you do want to do that, why do it in such a way that doctors will dismiss that possibility immediately?"

"I think you're reading too much into this, Lemming," Bradford said.

Lemming shook his head. "No, you're not reading enough into it."

The door opened and a woman's face poked through. "Inspector. 187 On the fourth street high rise. Two dead, one injured."

The inspector and detective Davis grabbed their jackets and headed out the door. The inspector looked back at Lemming. "What are you going to do?"

Lemming was still sitting down. He propped his legs up on the table and grinned.

"Find a guy named John Kirby," he said. "Mind if I have this apple?"

The door slammed shut.

October 23rd, 1990

Sandy Devereaux tossed the rest of her stale cinnamon bun into the trashcan. She really needed to start eating right, she thought to herself. She looked at herself in the hallway mirror. Was she getting fat? Whenever she was upset about anything, she ate. Damn Virginia for getting killed like that. She played with her long brown hair. No way was she getting fat and ruin those looks. No way. She'd start eating right tomorrow. Maybe she should start jogging. What was her ideal weight anyway? 120? 130? Suddenly her thoughts were interrupted as a tall, skinny girl walked out into the hall from a bedroom.

"Hey, Traci. Join me, I'm trying to will my weight away."

The girl laughed and went into the bathroom. She ran the water and applied some toothpaste to her brush. As she brushed her teeth, Sandy walked over to her and frowned.

"Look at you! You're wasting water! Run the water after you're through brushing!"

Traci McKinley shot her roommate a disgruntled look and kept on brushing.

"I have to get you to be more earth friendly, girl," Sandy said with an exasperated look on her face.

Traci rinsed and toweled off. "You know Sandy, you'll make a good mom someday."

"Oh shut up. I'm just trying to get you to care a little!"

"Are you sure you're not just upset about what happened next door?" Traci asked.

"Well, it's not often a girl you know gets murdered right next door to you. Aren't you scared?"

"No, not at all," Traci said, walking to the living room. She threw herself on the couch. "What's there to be scared about? I have no reason to be."

"Girl, have you ever heard the saying that a criminal often returns to the scene of the crime?"

Traci smiled and flicked on the television. "Why would he do that? This isn't some psycho you know. Virginia was killed by someone who was planning it for some reason."

Sandy was surprised. "How do you figure that?"

Traci turned to face her roommate. "Think about it. She was a calculating girl. I'd bet she was blackmailing someone. Probably some teacher she slept with. She was a whore you know."

"I know, but..."

There was a knock at the door. Sandy jumped as if startled. Traci shook her head. "Your nerves are shot babe. Answer that, will you?"

Sandy opened the door. An unshaven but pleasant looking man stood at the door. He smiled when he saw the girl.

"Miss Devereaux? Or are you Miss Traci?"

"I'm Sandy Devereaux. Can I help you?"

The stranger's eyes appraised the good looks of the young girl standing in front of him. He extended his hand.

"Miss Devereaux, it's a pleasure. My name is David Lemming, I'm a private investigator. May I come in?"

"Of course, I'm sorry," Sandy said, stepping aside. Lemming walked in and looked around.

"As I said, I'm an investigator. I was wondering..."

"If you could ask us a few questions about the murder next door?" Traci McKinley finished the sentence from her couch.

Lemming smiled and looked past Sandy to the thin girl on the couch.

"Yes, Miss McKinley. Mind if I sit down?" he said, pulling up a chair.

"How do you know our names?" Sandy asked.

Lemming looked at her carefully. Pretty, but shallow, he surmised. Probably was a cheerleader in high school. Now she's some sort of business major, and plans on sleeping her way to the top. He'd seen many Sandy Devereaux types in his life. On the other hand, Traci McKinley looked like an interesting girl. Her hair was matted and unwashed. He supposed that was the "in" look. Her skin was pale and freckled, as if she never got out much. She wore drabby, dark clothes. Miss counterculture, he thought, smiling to himself. However, she was smart, and possibly dangerous.

"I'm a detective, Miss Devereaux. Knowing things is my business."

"Oh!"

"What do you want to know?" Traci asked, looking straight into his eyes.

"Were you here around five or six p.m. on the 21st?"

"I was, Sandy was not."

"Did you hear anything?"

"Yes, I heard cars going by, the tv playing, kids yelling."

Lemming frowned. "I meant, anything from next door."

"No."

"You heard nothing?"

"That's right."

"How well did you know Miss Kelly?"

Traci McKinley turned off the tv. "I didn't know her well at all. I am friends with her roommate Amy though."

"I think they were both out that that night," Sandy spoke up.

Lemming kept looking right at Traci McKinley. "You're sure you heard nothing?"

Did she look a little nervous or was that his imagination?

"I heard nothing. I was reading a book or something."

Lemming kept staring at her, trying to read her thoughts. She was holding back something, all right.

"Isn't that strange, Miss McKinley? A murder occurs next door to you, with only a thin wall separating you from her, and you hear nothing?"

The girl's face was stone. "Look, Mr. Lemming, I'm not a stupid girl. This person who killed Virginia would kill again, if you know what I mean."

"You're right, he would if threatened by something," Lemming said slowly. "Do you know something that could be threatening to this person?"

"I've already told you, I heard nothing."

"Did you know the girl's fiancé, Joe Thurman?"

"I didn't know him, I saw him a couple of times."

Lemming straightened in his chair and leaned forward. "What's your impression of him?"

"I have no impression of anyone. I try not to judge people."

"I think he's a jerk," Sandy chimed in.

Lemming continued to look at Traci, trying to read her thoughts.

"Miss McKinley, I find it hard to believe that you had no impression of the guy."

"That's your problem."

Lemming smiled. "Miss McKinley, do you have any idea who killed Miss Kelly on the evening of October the 21st?"

Traci got up to shut the window shades. Then she turned to face Lemming.

"No, Mr. Lemming, I do not. And you want to know something else? I don't care."

Cool bitch, thought Lemming. She knows something, but won't tell. He got up and fumbled for his business card. Drawing one out, he handed it to Traci.

"If you want to talk, call me," he said. "Good day, ladies."

They said nothing as he walked out the door. He got in his car and smiled to himself. The skies were clouding up as he drove off. She'll call, he thought, guiding his old Chevy down the road. She'll call.

☠

Four Years Later...

Monday, April 16th, 1994

Mark Kane parked his silver Volvo in his parking spot. It was a dark and rainy day in Denver, and on days like this, he wished he would have hurried up and changed his tires. The car had hydroplaned twice getting him to work, and he had almost plowed into the back of a semi. He switched the car off and looked into his rear view mirror. His hair was a mess, so he took his hand and tried to brush it back in place. Why didn't he carry a damn brush? Like this will do any good. As soon as I race across this parking lot to the front door I'll get soaking wet. He stopped thinking about it and looked at his watch. 7:55 a.m. Good, he was early. Now he had time to face this torrential downpour. He grabbed his briefcase and opened the door making sure to lock it as he slid out. Slamming the door shut, he started running towards the front door of KBATech International, his place of work. He was halfway there when a sickening thought struck him. He had left his keys in the car, and now it was locked. He turned around slowly and realized that he had also left his lights on.

"Shit!"

Oh well, not much he could do now. He ran towards the building and rushed in. The secretary, Barbara, was there at her desk, looking as sweet as she always did. How did she manage to never get wet?

"Morning Mr. Kane," she greeted cheerfully.

"Morning Barbara," Kane grumbled and plodded into his office. He threw his briefcase down on his desk, which was already full of papers and other junk he had not thrown away. I'm a damn pack rat, he thought to himself. He sat down at his chair and looked at a memo on his desk. He read it and frowned.

KBATech was an international manufacturer of pressure inducers, digital systems, and other high accuracy test and measurement components. Located in Denver, it was a good central location for the headquarters, which employed

22

approximately two thousand people. Kane, a project engineer, was a man with some clout in the engineering department, which consisted of thirty five male engineers, five quality managers, and as Kane liked to put it, two "token" women engineers. He never made it a secret that he viewed women as second-class engineers, even though their accomplishments were second to none. This attitude did not make him the most popular man with the women of the company.

Now as he finished reading his memo, he poured some coffee in his stained mug and picked up the phone. He dialed an extension.

"Yeah."

"Nate? Kane here. What's with this memo on my desk? Kerry wants to go ahead and ok the 067 washer? I distinctly need spring steel, and that washer is just a 1010. What the hell..."

"Listen, Kane. You're going to have to bite the bullet on this one. Production at Carlyle's is already three weeks behind. Bossman's not going to have us sit on our ass on this thing."

"Well shit Nate, when did quantity take place over quality around here? I tell you, that damn washer needs a tougher material. I..."

"Kane, it's no use yelling at me man. I know what you're saying, but there's bigger things going on. Look, let's do lunch today, I'll explain later."

Kane slammed down the receiver. Let's do lunch? Nate was a dork. He was not having a good morning. His wife was coming back from visiting her parents that afternoon. How was he going to pick her up with a dead battery and no jumper cables?

"Mark, you look real happy," a female voice interrupted his thoughts.

Kane smiled. He looked up and saw Donna Houseman, one of the production managers. She was standing at the door, with her legs crossed. His eyes ran up and down those legs appreciatively. Donna was his best friend from college, and could always make him feel better.

"Rotten morning, Donna. I locked my damn keys in the car, and left the lights on. Now Kerry and Nate tell me that the 067 is going ahead without the revision. It's my ass on the line here, but no one seems to give a damn about that."

23

"I've got some jumper cables, don't worry," Donna reassured him. "As for 067, what do you want to do? Delay further and get us a bad name with Carlyle? Nissan will be real pleased with that."

"But..."

"No buts, Mark. You've been an engineer here long enough to know that sometimes you gotta give a little. Nissan wants parts, and they don't care about the strength of some little washer anymore."

Kane sighed. She was right. She was always right.

"Have I been here that long?" he asked, grinning.

Donna counted on her hands. "You're forty three now, so you've been here fifteen years, old boy!"

"And if I remember correctly, you're forty tomorrow!" Kane said, laughing.

"Don't remind me," Donna said. "I don't feel forty though."

"You don't look it either," Kane said admiringly.

Donna Houseman was certainly an attractive woman. He had known her since their college days at Georgia Tech. They had met in their sophomore year in Calculus three. Their relationship had always been platonic, and sometimes he wondered why that's the way it happened. Kane smiled to himself. I guess it's not true what Billy Crystal said in that movie, he thought. A man can indeed be friends with a woman and not "do" her, even if she's attractive. She was more like a sister to him.

"I'll get Danny to jump your car in a few minutes. I know you have to pick up Becky at the airport today," Donna said.

She truly had a remarkable memory.

"Thanks, you're a lifesaver."

"No problem. By the way, Stu's called a meeting after lunch in the big room. I got a feeling it's something big. Around one o'clock," she said and turned to leave.

"A meeting? Monday? I know this is going to be bad news," Kane grunted.

"See you then," she said and shut the door behind her.

Stuart Flannigan was the president of KBATech. There were two things he hated most in his life. Smoking, and meetings. Thus, the entire company had a no smoking policy, and if a meeting was called, it was usually bad news. Kane picked up a pen

24

and started scribbling his agenda for the day on a piece of paper.

1. Ask Tony if hopper was in yet.
2. Call and make a doctors's appointment for Trish
3. Check on production on Univox's accelerometers.
4. See if Ruth made that call to Boyd. If not, kill the bitch.
5. Meeting

He smiled and looked at his paper. Ruth Mercer was his right hand "woman". If he wanted parts ordered and was busy, she could be counted on. He threw the pad in his drawer as his door opened and a very large man waddled in. Yes, "waddled" was the right word for the way Roy Drake walked, thought Kane. The man was about five foot four and weighed over two hundred and fifty pounds. He sat down. There was a frown on his face.

"What can I do for you today, Roy?"

Drake was a sales representative for American Tube, a tubing supplier to KBATech for many years.

"Kane, why did you guys do it? You know we've done a good job for you guys."

Kane was puzzled. "Do what?"

"Oh come on. I've worked with you for twelve years. Why are you bumping us out?"

Kane shrugged. "Well, we're just dropping the aluminum hook, it's only ten thousand a year in volume, Roy. I doubt if..."

Drake interrupted. "Kane, you aren't listening to me, are you? I asked why you're bumping us out, as in why you're dropping us all together!"

Something was wrong. If KBATech was bumping out American Tube, it was news to Mark Kane. He started playing with his pencil. He had to think of something to say.

"Well, um, Roy, it's like this. You see..."

"I didn't expect to be screwed by you, Kane."

"Listen, Roy. I really don't know..."

"Save it!" Drake said sharply. "You guys were seventy percent of my business, Kane. You're pretty much going to break me. You know, you need a change of pace. Maybe a few days in the Bahamas with your pretty wife. Maybe you'll see the beauty of life out there, soak the sun, and think to yourself, hey, it's pretty nice to have friends you can count on. Have a nice life!"

He strode out and slammed the door. Kane hastily dialed a

number on the phone.

"Randall here."

"Hey Randall, what the hell is up with American Tube? I just had that fat ass Roy Drake come in here and bitch at me for screwing him over, and I don't even know what the..."

"You didn't hear? Stu canceled their account."

"No shit, I gathered that. Why?"

"He says they're getting stagnant. It's time to go with a newer, younger, fresher company. He wants Micrometals."

"Micrometals? Stu said that?"

"So I understand. Ask him at the meeting."

Kane hung up and stared at the ceiling. Yes, that would be consistent with recent happenings. Stu has recently been on this bolder, fresher, newer ideas kick. Ever since Clinton got elected to the white house, Stu has been Mr. idealist. Kane didn't share his views. It was not good for the company, as far as he was concerned. Dropping valuable and reliable vendors was never a good idea. He knew the price of being branded a company that cannot commit. It was like being divorced two or three times, no one wanted a relationship with you. He looked at his watch. It was nine forty five.

After having an uneventful lunch at the company cafeteria with Donna, Kane decided to visit Marty Finley, one of the product engineers. As he walked into his office, he noticed a picture of his five-year-old daughter Elise, on his wall. She had been diagnosed with leukemia last year. Ever since, Marty had not been the same joyful man. Kane couldn't blame him, knowing how he felt about his own kids.

"Hi Mark, what's up?"

"A lot, apparently," Kane said, shutting the door. "You heard any previews on this meeting?"

"Well word is that Stu's going to announce some sort of new job that we got. It's pretty hush, hush."

Kane's eyebrows shot up. Stu never called meetings to announce new jobs, so this surprised him.

"That's it?"

"I think so. I'm surprised too."

"What's gotten into Stu lately?" Kane said. "He's been Mr.

change hasn't he?"

"Uh-huh. Guess since he's the boss, he can do so. Say, I want to invite you to bring James and Trish over to Elise's fifth birthday party this Saturday."

"Of course. What time?"

"Six."

"We'll be there. How is she doing?"

Finley's face clouded. "It's day to day. Things are, you know, not good. The outlook is bleak."

Kane patted his shoulder. He really felt sorry for him. He couldn't imagine what he would do if James or Trish had something happen to them.

"Hang in there."

At about one o 'clock, Kane walked into the big meeting room. All of management and engineering was already there. This was big, he thought to himself, trying to find a seat. He finally grabbed a loose chair and sat down. Stuart Flannigan was standing at the podium and waiting for people as they filed in. Soon, the room was packed. Kane looked around. Donna was seated ten rows away. He flashed her a smile. She smiled back.

"I guess everyone's here so I am going to begin," Stuart Flannigan's loud voice boomed. "You all know I hate meetings so this will be short. I have called you all here to tell you about our merger."

There were some murmurs and talk among the crowd. Kane looked at Donna again. She looked back at him with an "I didn't expect this" glance.

"Let me just say that we have merged with Curry Enterprises, based in Los Angeles," Flannigan continued. "They are, as you know, the largest manufacturer of earth moving machines and building demolition tools in the world. They have offices in Honolulu, San Francisco, Atlanta, Nashville, Abilene, Toronto, London, Marseilles, Hong Kong, Delhi, Osaka, Sydney, and Djakarta. This is a truly international company we are merging with, and I believe it's a great move for us. They plan to build three more plants by the year 2000 in Cheyenne, Rome, and Munich. It gives me great pleasure in introducing to you the president of Curry Enterprises, Mr. Craig Phillips."

Applause broke out as a middle-aged man in an Armani suit strode up to the podium. The break allowed Kane time to think. This was not bad news after all. No wonder Stu had let American Tube go. He didn't need their inflated prices anymore with Curry's connections. Micrometals was a much bigger organization with a wider range of resources. His respect for Stu grew. Kudos to him for thinking big. Maybe he was a man of greater vision than he had given him credit for. He began to smile as Craig Phillips spoke. He looked over at Donna again. She was not looking at him, but listening intensely to the speaker. He leaned back in his chair. Everything was going to be all right.

This was going to be a great week.

He had no way of knowing how wrong he was.

Around five in the afternoon, as he was getting ready to leave, Kane's phone beeped. He picked it up.

"Kane here."

"Kane? Nate here. We were supposed to do lunch today, where did you disappear to?"

Shit. He had forgotten about the 067 part, the lunch, and Carlyle.

"I forgot, sorry. Listen; let's work it in tomorrow, ok? I have to go pick up Becky at the airport, and her plane lands in forty five minutes."

"All right. Tomorrow then."

"Deal."

"What's your opinion of this merger, Kane?"

"Love it. Growth is always good."

"Wonder if we can handle it."

"Nate, I'm surprised at you, I thought you can handle anything!" Kane said, laughing.

"Shut up," Nate said, laughing. "Listen, I have to run too. I'll see you tomorrow. Stay out of trouble."

At that moment, Kane did not know how much meaning those words carried.

☠

A Drink With A Stranger

Kane drove along I-70 toward the airport. He made a mental note to thank Danny, the maintenance foreman, for unlocking his car and giving him a jump. He was glad his wife was coming home after two weeks. He had missed her. The kids had missed her, especially in the cooking department. He couldn't believe that a six and an eleven year old could get sick of pizza, but after a week, even he longed for his wife's cooking. As he turned off onto the airport exit, he realized that he was about twenty minutes early. He parked the Volvo and walked into the airport. The Delta Airlines booth was not far away, and he saw that his wife's flight was delayed due to bad weather at Memphis. He went up to the lady at the booth.

"Excuse me, I noticed flight 1673 from Memphis is late, could you tell me when it'll be in?"

"It's running about forty minutes late. I'd say it'll be in about 6:30," the lady said, smiling.

Thanking the lady, Kane decided that he would go to the lounge for a drink. It had been a long day and he longed for a nice bourbon. He looked up at the sign in front of the lounge entrance.

MILE HIGH BAR

How quaint. Everything in this city was mile high this and mile high that, he thought as he sat down at a stool. Denver was a very ordinary city. It wasn't "wild" like Los Angeles, or "Hip" like Seattle. It wasn't even "windy" like Chicago, or "Hot" like Atlanta. It was just there, in the middle of Colorado, in the middle of America. Colorado was such an uninteresting state to him. It's shape was even uninteresting, just a plain rectangle. It boasted the city that had lost three Super Bowls in a row. A city mired, in fact, in mediocrity. A city, which had to get its nickname by merely being five thousand feet above sea level. No, he did not like Denver, and longed to return to Atlanta, back to his good old

29

college days. His wife on the other hand, loved Denver. She would, she was from Montana, an even more desolate state.

"What'll it be?" the fat black man with the ferocious handlebar moustache asked from behind the bar.

"Bourbon and Coke. Easy on the rocks."

The bartender quickly poured his drink and set it in front of him. Kane took a sip and sighed.

"Rough day?"

Kane smiled. "Aren't they all?"

"Just thought I'd ask. It's my job you know."

Kane took another sip of his drink and looked around. There was only one other person at the bar; a man, sitting a few stools to his left. As Kane looked right at him, he noticed that the man was looking right back at him.

"Evening," the man said cheerfully.

"Evening."

"Here to pick someone up, or leaving our fair city?"

"Picking up my wife," Kane said, mixing his drink with his stirrer.

"Ah, I figured you were a married man," the man said, extending his hand. "My name's Kirby. John Kirby. I'm here to pick up my gal too. She's coming back from Elvistown."

"Oh, then she's probably on the same flight as my wife," Kane said. "Your wife's an Elvis fan?"

"My girlfriend," Kirby corrected, "And yea, I think she still believes he's still alive."

"I just saw him working a lunch counter down there," Kane said, laughing. "My name's Kane. Mark Kane."

"Nice to meet you Mark," Kirby said politely. "So what do you do around here?"

"I'm an engineer at KBATech. What about you?"

Kirby took a sip of his beer. "I'm what's known in the business as a professional womanizer," he said, with a wink.

Kane grinned. The man was playing around. He decided to humor him.

"Come again?"

"A professional womanizer."

"And that would involve...?"

"Oh I basically seduce women, stay with them for a few

30

months. I'm doing that with my current one," Kirby said bringing his face nearer to Kane and lowering his voice. "After that, it's on to another one. Of course I milk them for all they got."

Was this guy for real? Kane stared at John Kirby. The man was not really good looking, fairly average height, average build, average face, average moustache, and average body. In fact, the only thing that struck him about this man was his incredible averageness - other than his ego, of course. There was also something not all there. The man was fake in some manner.

He smiled and responded noncommittally. "How are the benefits of this, um... career?"

Kirby did not detect the sarcasm. "Benefits are great. No retirement package, but who wants to retire from this job?"

Kane started to be bored. "You're so right."

"Yes," Kirby whispered. "Let me get you in on a little secret. All men should live this way. Treat women like the bitches they are. They do it to men all the time. It's time us men turn the tables."

John Kirby was a real champion for women's liberation.

Kane looked at the bottle of Bud Light in Kirby's hand. "How many of those have you had?"

Kirby chuckled. "You think I'm drunk and babbling? Not so, my friend. I speak my mind to you, because you're a stranger. Let's face it, we'll probably never see each other again, so it's safe for me to reveal my secret to you. You won't go telling anyone I know."

"Don't you think you may get blacklisted or stalked by some girl who may not take it all that well?"

Kirby shook his head in mock despair. "Don't you think I've already run into that problem? I have my way of dealing with them."

"Oh, really? What do you do?"

Kirby grinned. It was an evil grin, the type of grin that exposes a man's true inner being.

"I get rid of them," he said simply.

"Excuse me?"

"I get rid of them," Kirby repeated, his grin intact.

"Would you care to explain?" Kane pressed on.

Kirby's face suddenly underwent a metamorphosis. It

31

clouded and became somewhat unwilling.

"I can't explain any further. You figure it out."

Kane had the feeling that the man was playing a part in some movie. He half expected Oliver Stone or Barry Levinson to yell, "Cut! Too dramatic!" He was getting tired of this strange man. He looked at his watch. It was six twenty.

"Oh look, my wife's plane's about to land," he said, getting up. "It was nice meeting you."

Kirby said nothing and kept sipping his beer. Kane downed the rest of his bourbon and Coke and threw down a five-dollar bill. He went out of the bar, thinking that he had just met a very suspicious character. He looked back. The bartender was looking at him. Kirby was still drinking his beer. A very suspicious character indeed.

By the time Kane first saw his wife emerge out of gate sixteen, it was six fifty five. He ran up to take her handbag, throwing his arms around her and planting a kiss on her lips. She looked tired.

"I missed you."

"I missed you too honey. How were the kids?"

"They're fine, but starving," Kane said, laughing as they walked down to baggage claim. "They miss their mommy."

Rebecca Kane smiled, showing a set of perfect white teeth that contrasted sharply with her dark hair. "I missed them. Mom and dad are fine, but they asked me to tell you to lose weight. They saw your pictures."

Kane patted his stomach as they waited on the conveyor to start. "I'm not that bad off hon. You should see some guys at the office that are my age."

"Silly!" Becky Kane said, laughing. " I was kidding. I wouldn't show them those horrible pictures."

Kane playfully shoved his wife as the conveyor started. The suitcases began to crash down the chutes. Out of the corner of his eye, he noticed John Kirby, the man he had met at the bar. He was sitting at a chair against the wall. There was no girl with him. He had a bag lying next to his chair. Kane studied the man carefully for a second time. From time to time, he liked to play a game with himself. He would try to hone his detective skills by observing someone and try to deduce things about that person. Looking at

Kirby, one thing immediately leaped out at him. There was no way this man was a ladies man, like he had claimed to be. He was more likely to be a dentist, or maybe even a lawyer. Perhaps he was a small time criminal, even. For that matter, he could be a cop. He looked more carefully at his clean-cut hairdo, and realized that it was too clean cut. It had to be a wig. The man was probably bald, or balding. His suspicion grew. He must be very insecure to wear such a wig. Either that or he was in disguise for some reason. He wore brown pants and a grey T-shirt. His jacket was blue, with no distinguishable marks on it. The man was definitely lacking in style and taste, not to mention originality.

"Who are you staring at, honey?" his wife asked.

Kane came to with a start. "Oh, just daydreaming. Did I tell you we're merging with Curry?"

"Curry?"

"Curry Enterprises, one of the largest industrial demolition and heavy equipment manufacturers in the world. This could mean some big bonuses, not to mention our stock in KBATech jumping."

"That's great! I'm longing to get back to work myself, Mark. I miss it."

Becky was a weatherwoman at a local television station. She had recently gone back to school and gotten her degree in meteorology. He often kidded her that it was the most inexact science in the world, but secretly he was quite proud of her. One of these days, he would tell her so.

"There's my suitcase. Come on, grab it and let's go."

Kane picked up her grey suitcase and wheeled it outside, with his wife opening doors for him. Outside, the rain was letting up, and it was getting dark.

"Ooh, honey, you know something?" Becky exclaimed. "I can tell the difference in the air."

"I know, it's thinner," Kane said in a bored voice as he started the car. His wife looked at him with a knowing look.

"What's with the tone of voice? You haven't been on your "Denver's such a boring city" kick again, have you?"

Kane had to smile in spite of himself. His wife knew him too well. After fourteen years of marriage, she should.

"So how's Donna?" she asked, changing the subject.

Kane pondered on that one. Becky had never gotten along very well with Donna Houseman. He supposed that she was somewhat jealous of her friendship with him. She would never admit this was the case, though. With Becky, things that were unpleasant were better left not discussed. What was funny was, she had a lot in common with Donna.

"She's fine. Kept me from being bored stiff while you were gone."

As soon as he said it, he wished he hadn't. Becky's dark eyes flashed, and she had set her jaw. This was trouble.

"Did she?" she said in a calm voice. "And what did you two do?"

Okay say the right thing, idiot. Don't let her get angrier for nothing.

"Well, she came over sometimes, and we'd rent movies, sometimes go out dancing, or..."

"Dancing? You don't even like dancing."

Wrong answer. Idiot. Kane wanted to kick himself.

"Well, it's ok. I like the way you dance better," he said, in a flash of brilliance. There. That should calm her down.

"Mark, I think you and Donna are a little too close."

Kane turned his head to look at his wife. "What are you trying to say?"

"I'm saying, you're a married man. It doesn't look good for you to be so close to another woman who's not your wife. Especially not when your wife's in another city."

"Honey, is that jealousy rearing its ugly head?"

"No, no!" Becky said, shaking her head a little too vigorously. "But people might think it's weird. People who don't know you."

Kane grunted. "Who cares what people who don't know me think about me?"

"Mark, it's not that," Becky said in a matter of fact tone. "It's just that you should keep an image."

"Honey, I'm not going to turn my back on a twenty three year friendship just because she's female, I'm married to another woman, and people might talk. Let's just say I'm not that shallow."

Becky didn't say anything, but Kane could tell she was still angry. She gets pissed at the stupidest things sometimes, he

34

thought. He decided to soothe her feelings.

"Listen, hon. If it'll make you feel any better, she's got a boyfriend. I'll invite them both over for dinner tomorrow night, it's her birthday tomorrow anyway. You'll see that she's all right. You might even like her."

"Well, okay," Becky said, warming up to the idea. "Mark, it's not that I am jealous. I just want us to be closer."

Kane leaned over and kissed her earlobes. "We are close, honey."

As he turned into the driveway of their two-story house in Glendale, he noticed that the lights were on.

"I had Nadine pick up the kids. I guess she's still here."

Nadine Long was Becky's cousin. She was a great lady, Kanc thought, to do the many errands she did for them. As he unlocked the house and went in, he heard footsteps coming down the stairs.

"Mommy! Dad!" It was their six-year-old son, James. He was followed by his pretty eleven-year-old daughter, Trish.

"Hi mom! How was Memphis?"

Becky Kane hugged her children. She had indeed missed them.

"Memphis was great, kids! It was sunny almost the whole time, and gramma and grandpa missed you guys!"

"I wish I could have gone," James said wistfully.

Nadine Long came out of the kitchen, smiling. She was a fifty four year old woman who looked like a grandma in every way. Her graying hair fell across her dark eyes. She threw her arms around Becky.

"Welcome back sweetheart. I thought you guys might be hungry, so I threw a pot roast in the oven."

"You threw a pot roast in the oven?" Kane said, laughing. "Come on Nadine, that took some time."

"Well, I had a little time," Nadine admitted, smiling.

"You're staying for dinner, right?" Becky asked.

"No, no, I promised George that I'd take him bowling tonight, and I'll be late if I stay any longer. I'd better go."

"Ok hon. Thanks again. Drive carefully!" Becky said.

Nadine put her jacket on and left. Kane threw his wife's suitcase on the sofa and crashed down next to it.

"It has been one long day!"

His wife curled down next to him and started playing with his curly brown hair.

"Kids, will you set the table please!" Kane yelled, and then looked at Becky. "Sorry for being a little short with you in the car."

"That's okay," she said, putting a finger to his lips. "Let's forget about it."

She buried her head in his chest. Kane Started playing with her ears. "You know, I just found out Trish has a boyfriend."

Becky looked up at him in surprise.

"It's that Johnny DaMento kid," Kane continued. "His dad's a doctor you know."

Becky looked skeptical. "Dr. DaMento?"

"Why not?" Kane was chuckling.

Becky sighed. "Well, she's eleven. I guess it's time for her infatuations."

"So you're okay with it?"

"Are you?"

"Yeah," Kane said slowly. "She's growing. It's only natural I guess."

"I bet you had many girlfriends when you were eleven," Becky said playfully.

"I hated girls when I was eleven," Kane said, getting up from the sofa. "Let's eat."

"Okay, but you know what's for dessert?"

Kane grinned. "Surprise me."

Tuesday, April 17th, 1994

Chief Chandler Davis looked suspiciously at the girl that was shown into his office. He had only been Chief for three months, and he had not gotten the job the way he had wanted it. His good friend Hal Bradford had been killed in the line of duty, and he had been next in line. Now, as the tall, skinny girl with matted brown hair sat down in front of him, he let his past experience as a detective rise to the surface. The girl was not impressive to the sight.

"Good morning Miss McKinley. Detective Walker said you had an urgent matter to discuss with me?"

The girl looked pale and nervous. She bit her lips.

"Mind if I smoke?"

"Go ahead," Davis said, pushing the ashtray towards her.

She lit a cigarette and took a puff. It seemed to calm her down.

"You're right. It is an urgent matter," she said, exhaling a cloud of smoke.

Davis said nothing. The girl continued.

"I think my life is in danger."

Davis did not flinch. A great many paranoid people came to him with the same story.

"Go on," he said calmly.

"Okay," Traci McKinley said, taking a deep breath. "I'm a nurse at General. I had the day off today. This morning, I went out to get the newspaper. A car drove by and I saw someone pointing a gun at me. I ducked down behind a car, and the bullet missed me. I looked up to see the car speeding away."

"Did you get a look at the individual?"

"Not really. It was a white man, though. I'm sure of that."

The chief jotted this down. "What kind of car was it?"

"It was brown. I'm not good at recognizing cars. I think it was a Toyota."

37

The chief sighed. "Miss McKinley, that's not much to go on. Did you get a license number?"

"Oh sure, as I was flying through the air avoiding bullets, I magically pulled out a sheet of paper and jotted it down with the aid of my x-ray eyes and magic pen."

Chief Davis did not appreciate the sarcasm. He ran his hand through his hair and looked down at his desk.

"I'll be frank Miss McKinley. Without any clues, I cannot..."

The girl interrupted him. "I just want some police protection, that's all."

Davis's eyes narrowed. "Do you have some reason to believe that your life is in jeopardy? This was not a freak gang related shooting?"

The girl shook her head. "This was no freak shooting. I'm not in a gang. I was a target, for some reason."

"What reason?"

"I'm not sure," Traci McKinley was nervous again." I think I may have witnessed something."

Davis leaned forward. "Witnessed what?"

McKinley bit her lip. "I'm not sure, really. Will you give me protection?"

"Miss McKinley, this city doesn't have enough policemen to keep up with the crime. I can't just devote a cop for you unless it's a serious situation."

McKinley got angry. Her voice rose. "Serious situation! Chief, some guy took a potshot at me with a gun from a speeding car. What do you call that? Some kind of joke? Well, Chief Davis, I am not laughing!"

The girl was holding back something, Davis thought. Yet she may just be another publicity seeker, or some paranoid girl with a persecution complex.

"I'll tell you what, Miss McKinley," he said slowly. "I'll have Officer Garrett patrol your street frequently tonight. What's your address?"

"723 Deerfield lane, apartment one," the girl said. "Thank you chief, I really appreciate it."

Davis got up to shake her hand. She took it with a look of gratefulness.

38

"Miss McKinley, if you remember anything, let me know."

"I will," she said, leaving the office.

Davis sat back down and got lost in thought. In a few minutes a young Latino policeman came in, chuckling.

"Say, who was the flowerchild, sir?"

"Nurse at General. Thinks her life is in danger."

"She drives a Porsche. Nice car for a nurse. Bet her folks are loaded."

Davis smiled. "Maybe she's your calling, Montoya. You always wanted to marry a rich girl."

"Yeah, that would be nice. Sit back, raise kids, and let her bring home the bacon. Wouldn't hurt my male ego a bit."

Davis crossed his arms and leaned back in his seat. "You're a regular nineties man."

"Too bad she looks like a damn hippie."

Davis sighed. "Don't you have work to do, Montoya?"

"Yes sir," Montoya said and ducked out.

Davis couldn't get back to his thoughts. His phone rang.

"Davis here."

"Chief Davis? I would like to talk to you." It was a deep male voice.

"That's what you're doing, bud."

"I am very concerned."

"Who is this?"

"I'm a friend of the girl who just walked out of your office." The voice had a slight southern twang to it.

"What girl would that be?"

"A Miss Traci McKinley. Interested?"

Davis was puzzled. He spoke into the speaker slowly. "What's your concern with all of this?"

"Listen to me chief," the voice grew impatient, "The girl knows what she's talking about. You really have to believe her."

"I'm not sure what you're talking about."

"Let's stop playing games, Chief," the man was getting weary. "I think she needs protection."

"From what?"

"Someone tried to kill her!"

"How do you know all of this? Who the hell are you anyway?"

"My name's not important! I know something, and so does she. She's living in fear."

Davis started to feel agitated. "Look if you'll explain what you have..."

"I'm serious!" The phone went dead.

"Hello? Hello? Damn!" The chief slammed down the receiver and started muttering to himself. The office door opened, and officer Marlon Fisher poked his head through.

"Everything okay sir?"

"No, everything is not okay. Who's been giving out my private office phone number?"

"Well sir, all a person has to do is dial information and..."

"Forget it, it was a rhetorical question. Listen Fisher, did you see that girl that was in here earlier?"

"Oh, yes sir."

"Your impression of her?"

Fisher smiled. "She was cute sir, if you like tall, skinny, breast-less women."

"Why do I waste my time!," Davis said disgustedly. "Get out!"

Fisher marched out, smiling. Davis got up and put his jacket and hat on. He was not going to let these silly distractions bother him. The girl was a paranoid freak, and that's all there was to it. He looked at his watch. It was almost lunchtime. He had time to pay an old friend a visit.

In fifteen minutes time, Chief Davis was knocking at the door of a Law office in downtown Denver.

"Come on in." The voice was raspy.

The chief opened the door and walked in. He smiled acknowledgement at the man behind the desk. Donald Watts was on the phone. He motioned with his free hand for him to sit down. Davis did so, and looked around the office. There were University degrees on the wall. Some newspaper clippings were posted up on the side of a filing cabinet. One headline in particular caught his eye.

24 YEAR OLD GRAD STUDENT
SLAIN IN HER APARTMENT

The article was dated October 22nd, 1990. It was about the murder of a young psychology graduate student named Virginia Kelly. Davis reflected back to that time and remembered the event. He remembered a nervous but dangerous man named Joe Thurman. He remembered David Lemming, the arrogant private dick. What was he doing these days? He had lost touch with the man. He reflected further on how evidence from the case was gathered, and the total lack of clues there had been. Even a motive was difficult to find. Eventually a man named Michael Barnard was accused of the murder. He had been a drug supplier to the dead girl. Of course he was acquitted because of a lack of evidence. His body was found in the gutter the next month in a drug related shooting. Indeed, if you live by the sword, you die by the sword. He remembered that the case was finally marked down to a drug related hit and marked as "unsolved." He looked at the man in front of him, still talking on the phone. Donald Watts had been the prosecuting attorney on the case. For weeks he had tried to convict Barnard on a drug deal gone bad. He had tried for first-degree murder, but had failed to even get manslaughter. There had been simply no evidence. The case fizzled away, but Donald Watts had apparently not forgotten it, as was evident by the headline on his cabinet.

Finally, Watts put the phone down and got up to shake Davis's hand.

"Chandler! How nice to see you again. How long has it been?"

"A couple of years," Davis said sheepishly.

Watts sat back down, relaxed. "So what brings you to my little corner of the world?"

Davis smiled. "Would you believe, nostalgia?"

"Nostalgia?"

"Well, I was sitting in my office, going out of my mind. I thought, hey, let's pay my old friend Don Watts a visit and talk about old times."

Watts laughed. "Chandler, you know it's a sure sign you're getting old when you want to talk about old times!"

Davis pointed to the newspaper clipping. "I noticed you still think about old times."

Watts sighed. "You know, I have never been very satisfied with that case."

"What's to be satisfied about? He got away."

"Well, he got what he deserved, but that's not what I mean," Watts said. "I'm talking about the guy who killed her, not who sold the drugs to her. I never was convinced Barnard did it."

"And yet you tried like hell to convict him for it," Davis said, shaking his head. "You lawyers are all alike."

"It's my job, Chandler."

"I guess so. I agree with you, too. I was very frustrated with the case myself," Davis said listlessly. "Get this. Today, this girl comes into my office saying she's been shot at. She claims she's afraid for her life. I get these crackpots all the time, but..."

"...but you think she's different?"

"Exactly. I have a funny feeling about it. This McKinley girl had some type of vibe that was just hard to ignore," Davis said. "And after she left, some guy calls me up to warn me that she shouldn't be ignored. He doesn't identify himself, and hangs up."

"McKinley?" Watts was frowning. "That name seems to ring a bell."

Davis leaned forward. "You're getting the same feeling? "

"Uh huh. Name sounds familiar, but I can't recall..." Watts broke off, thinking.

"Why don't we go by Richie's and grab a burger?" Davis suggested. "Maybe it'll revive our brains."

"Good idea. Let me get my jacket."

Richie's was an informal cafe on Farley Avenue, and the two men got there during the lunch hour. The place was always busy, and waiters were whisking by, carrying trays of food expertly. Chief Davis liked to come here for lunch frequently. The food was good, the service was fast, the waiters were courteous, and the beer was always cold. The two men were seated by a perky hostess, who no doubt was a local college student. The place did have an air of counterculture to it, but Davis didn't mind. He excused himself to go to the bathroom as Watts read his menu. He walked over to the men's room, and as he was about to open the door, it opened inward and a man walked out. Davis recognized him immediately.

"Mr. David Lemming. How the heck are you doing?" he

greeted the man cheerfully.

The man looked at him a second and then broke into a smile. "Detective Davis! I haven't worked with you in a while! Why is it always detective Walker I always work with now?"

"Well, I'm Chief Davis now."

"Well congratulations! Let me buy you a drink!"

The chief looked over at his table. "Well, why don't you just join me and Don for lunch?"

Lemming looked over at their table and thought it over for a minute. Then he relented.

"Sure. We can discuss old cases, catch up some."

"That's my friend Don Watts at the table," Davis explained. "You go over and join him, I'll be right with you two."

When he came back from the bathroom, Watts and Lemming were in deep conversation.

"I have to disagree, Don," Lemming was saying, "I really think that Hillary's an admirable first lady."

"Oh please," Watts retorted. "She thinks she's the president."

Davis sat down. "I see you two have gotten acquainted."

"Acquainted?" Watts was somewhat incredulous. "I've known David here for years, Chandler."

"I forget about Mr. Lemming's name here in Denver," Davis said.

The waiter came over. Lemming immediately spoke up. "Get all three of us a whiskey and club soda for starters."

"I really shouldn't drink the hard stuff," Davis objected weakly. "I'm on duty you know."

"Duty schmuty. Come on. Live a little. No one will kill you for having one drink."

Davis relented. "What the hell."

The meal was a good one, and the three spent most of it in silent appreciation of food. Finally, Donald Watts spoke up.

"You know David, Chandler and I were discussing that Virginia Kelly murder case four years ago. You remember that?"

Lemming took a sip of his drink. "How could I forget? It was one of my first unsolved cases."

"Well now, technically it was not your case, Mr. Lemming. It was mine," Davis corrected.

Lemming shook his head in disagreement. "No, it was mine as well. The girl's parents hired me."

Watts wiped his mouth. "Boy, what a frustrating case it was, too."

Lemming sighed. "I know. So many loose ends not connected. So many leads I couldn't begin to decipher."

Davis eyed Lemming. "You always suspected her fiancé didn't you? That guy Joe Thurman?"

Lemming chuckled. "Yeah, I think he may have committed the perfect murder. He left no clues to connect him, and he never bragged about it to anyone. Most killers give themselves away by bragging about it to their friends, usually in a drunken stupor at some bar. Not him. Of course he had the motive, since I believe he was in love with another woman."

Davis nodded. "Yes, it's usually human nature to not be able to keep secrets. Almost always a killer will tell someone about what he did."

"What about the Kelly girl?" Watts asked. "Didn't she sleep around too?"

Lemming's face got serious. "She was a drug user. I'd say she did what she had to for her drugs."

Davis rubbed his hands together. "You know who I suspected? I always thought it was her brother, that Scott Kelly character."

Watts looked surprised. "What? What possible..."

"I think he came down that day to kill her. Wasn't it a coincidence that..."

"Wait, wait, wait," Lemming interrupted him. "Scott Kelly tried to beat the hell out of Michael Barnard on the steps of the courthouse. You think that he would kill..."

"Listen to my motive," Davis broke in. "I found out Scott Kelly was adopted. When I spoke with their parents, I found out that Scott had a little "crush" on his sister. They actually sent the boy to therapy. Suppose he was jealous? Suppose he was jealous, and if he couldn't have her, no one could?"

Lemming laughed. "Man, that is just too sick."

"Is it? Scott was adopted at age sixteen. It's possible for him to be infatuated with his newly acquired older "sister". Virginia Kelly was a fairly good looking girl."

44

"We're all just speculating, guys," Watts interjected. " The fact is, with no evidence, we really have no idea who killed the girl. It might have been green men from Pluto for all we know."

Lemming set his plate aside and sniffed. "It was Thurman. I'd bet my life on it."

Davis studied David Lemming's face. The arrogance was showing through again. He really couldn't blame him. After all, with a success rate like his, one could afford to be arrogant. He shifted his thoughts to other things, and looked out the window. The sun was shining brightly now.

"Looks like good weather outside."

"Yes, they said it would get up to sixty today," Watts said. "I may leave early and get in some golf."

David Lemming got to his feet. "Well gentlemen, thank you for lunch. I'm afraid I can't play golf. I have work to do. It was a pleasure."

He walked out of the cafe and got into his car, parked right in front of the building. Davis noted that he was parked illegally, but had no ticket on his windshield. As he drove off, Watts made a face.

"Can you believe that? Who invited him to play? And what gave him the idea we were paying for his lunch?"

Davis wasn't listening. He was looking out the window. Now, he came to with a start. " What?"

"Nothing. What planet are you on?"

Davis smiled. "No, I was just wondering why a big time hot shot P.I. like him drives a piece of shit like that."

"Well, he's a democrat," Watts joked. "He probably doesn't believe in reckless spending."

Davis got up. "Well Don, it was nice seeing you again. Say hello to your wife for me."

Watts was surprised. "You don't want a ride back to the station?"

"No, I know you're busy. I'll catch a cab."

"Always a pleasure, Chandler. Drop by anytime!"

The chief paid his bill and walked outside. The sidewalk was busy with people. IIe looked around for a cab. He was not fond of driving, and preferred to get around by way of public transportation. Soon, a cab stopped and he got in.

"Metropolitan P.D."

He sat back and relaxed as the cab rolled along. The day's events started to come into focus. He thought again about the nervous girl that had called on him earlier. Why could he not get her out of his mind? There was something about her name, something in the past. McKinley: Where had he heard that name before?

Suddenly he sat bolt upright. Of course! McKinley!

"Driver! Stop here!" He had spotted a phone booth.

"This is the middle of the road sir."

"Pull over. I'm a cop, it's okay."

The driver obliged, and Davis paid him quickly. He ran to the phone booth and looked at the directory.

"Let's see... McKinley, Traci. Here it is, 723 Deerfield Lane. 555-2649."

He dialed the number quickly.

"This is Traci. I'm sorry, but I'm out right now. If you'll leave a name and number, I will be sure to..."

Davis slammed the receiver down. "Damn!"

He looked around. A couple of people were staring at him. Ignoring them, he put another quarter in and dialed another number.

"Metropolitan Police Department. This is Terri," a female voice answered.

"Terri, it's Chief Davis. Is detective Walker around?"

"I'll see if he is, sir."

After being on hold for what seemed like an eternity, another voice spoke.

"Walker here."

"Matt. Listen, you remember that girl who called on me this morning?"

"Sure do, chief."

"Her name was Traci McKinley. She was involved in that 1990 Virginia Kelly murder case. Get Dunn and meet me at 723 Deerfield lane, apartment one."

"Sir, what's going on?"

"I don't have time to answer questions. Hurry up, someone's life may be in danger."

Walker got the point. "We'll be there in fifteen minutes sir."

46

"Make it ten!"

Davis hung up and looked at his watch. It was now two thirty. He now had a problem. How was he going to get there in time? He suddenly wished that he had driven. He wished even more that he had made that cab wait for him. There was only one thing to do. He looked around. A slim brunette was getting into a red Beretta with a bag of clothes. He ran over to her quickly and flashed his badge.

"Ma'am, I'm a cop. I need to use your vehicle."

The woman was surprised. "Where's yours?"

"Never mind where mine is," Davis said, hopping into the driver's seat. The woman grabbed his hand.

"No way! If you're taking my car, I'm coming with you."

"No chance," Davis said, looking around wildly. "Where are the damn keys?"

"They're hidden. I won't tell you unless you take me along."

"You're obstructing the law, lady!"

The woman refused to talk. Finally, Davis gave in.

"All right, you can come. But when we get there, you stay in the car!"

"Okay," she said, smiling. Her hand went to the ashtray and pulled out some keys.

"I never carry then with me."

Davis started up the car, put it into gear and sped forward. His companion looked at him. He glanced at her quickly. She was quite young, and quite attractive.

"Where are we going anyway?" she asked. "Aren't you driving a little too fast?"

"I am going to hopefully stop a girl from being killed," Davis said, emphasizing the word "I". " You are going nowhere!"

"That sounds exciting! This kind of thing has never happened to me before!"

"Happens to me all the time."

The girl grinned. "You must lead an exciting life. What's your name?"

"I'm Chief Chandler Davis," Davis said, forcing a smile. "Nice to meet you Miss..."

"Teresa Manley. I was just finishing some shopping."

"Nice to meet you," Davis said, swerving sharply to avoid

hitting a car.

"As I was saying, this must be an exciting job, being a cop and all!"

Davis tried to be social. "It has got its moments, but some of it involves stark reality. Reality I could do without."

"I'm a teller at first central bank. It's a really boring job."

Davis nodded. "Sometimes we have to do stakeouts. That's a really boring job."

Teresa Manley was stunned. "Stakeouts boring? I'd think they'd be wildly exciting!"

Davis chuckled. "What if you got robbed at your teller job? Would that be exciting enough for you?"

The girl was taken aback. She thought for a moment. "No, I don't think I'd like that too much. Watch out!"

A truck had pulled out right in front of their speeding car. Davis swerved into the oncoming lane and narrowly missed it. A passing car honked loudly in annoyance.

"You're driving a little fast," the girl said, a little breathlessly.

"Just trying to give you a little excitement," Davis said with a crooked grin on his face. He turned on to a street and slowed down. This was Deerfield Lane. He found the apartment complex he was looking for. Walker was already in front of apartment one with Officer Thomas Dunn. He double parked beside their cruiser and got out.

"Good, you guys made it."

"There's the apartment sir."

He looked at the Porsche 911 sitting outside the apartment. She was in.

"Good. She's here. Let's go talk to her."

The three policemen walked up to the door. Walker knocked. There was no answer.

"Miss McKinley? It's Chief Davis from downtown. Could we talk to you?"

There was still no answer. Davis tried to peek in through the window, but the shades were drawn. He tried the door, but it was locked.

"She must not be here sir," Walker spoke up.

"Her car's here."

"She may have left with someone."

"Maybe. We'd better break down the door."

Walker blinked. "Sir, I'm not sure that..."

"Do it! I'll take the responsibility."

Dunn looked under the welcome mat. "No need for any destruction. There's a key here."

Davis sighed. "What's with women and their keys? They don't like to carry them for some reason."

Walker unlocked the door and opened it. The three walked in slowly.

"Miss McKinley!"

The lights in the living room were on. The room was decorated sparsely, but tastefully. Davis went into the kitchen as Walker went upstairs. It was a townhouse type of apartment.

"What are we looking for, sir?" Dunn asked.

Davis was tense. "I don't know, son." He did not like the feeling he was getting in his stomach.

"She's a reader. Look at all these books," Dunn observed.

"Sir! Please come upstairs!" It was Walker.

Davis ran up the stairs to the bedroom Walker's voice had come from. He entered the room and froze. Detective Walker was standing over the bed in the middle of the room. It was a nice twin bed, and would sleep two comfortably, except there was only one person in it. It was Traci McKinley. There was a long, jagged knife sticking out of her lifeless throat.

49

Aftermath

The apartment was crawling with police. It was now four in the afternoon. Chief Davis stood by and watched as two people carted the dead body away. Walker had found her at about two-fifty. Dunn had called it in immediately. The press was not sleeping on the job, as they were now milling about as well. Davis did his best to avoid them, but it was pointless. Inevitably, a tall newswoman stuck a microphone in his face.

"Chief, is this a serial killer? Is there reason to be concerned?"

"At this point we do not know much, but there is always reason to be concerned whenever a murder occurs," he said diplomatically. He hated journalists with a passion.

"Chief, are there any suspects? Anyone in custody?"

"We have no leads at this moment, but we are working on it," he said, and brushed past the woman rudely. This was a horrible day. Davis looked out the window and sighed. He had been too late. If he had done something this morning, this might not have happened.

"Well, chief. We meet twice in one day," a familiar voice spoke behind him. Davis turned around to face a smiling David Lemming. He did not return the smile.

"Would you call it deja-vu, chief?" Lemming said annoyingly.

"I would call it irritating and tragic, Mr. Lemming."

Lemming's eyebrows shot up. "A girl is murdered, and you'd call it irritating, chief?"

Davis was not in the mood to chat. "What are you doing here, Mr. Lemming?"

Lemming surveyed the scene. "Well, what do you think I am doing here chief? Crime is my passion, and a crime has been committed. Let's just say, my passions are aroused."

"How very nice for you."

"Chief, what I meant by the deja-vu comment is, doesn't this whole scene seem a little familiar?"

Davis nodded. "Yes, I'd have to agree, the parallels are there."

"Well, we going to question Mr. Thurman again?"

Davis was taken aback. "You think Thurman..."

"Why not? I'm pretty sure he committed the first one. This one's either a copycat or the same guy."

Davis thought a moment. "Of course, after proper investigation, we do have to talk to the guy."

Lemming laughed. "Yes, and while you "properly" investigate, the guy hauls butt to Mexico, never to be seen from again. Chief, you gotta arrest him, now!"

Davis looked incredulous. "Mr. Lemming, we can't arrest someone for murder because we think he did it. We have to have a little more proof than the suspicions of a local detective."

Lemming gestured with his hands. "Okay, give me some details here. What happened?"

"We found her at two fifty this afternoon. Doctor says she hadn't been dead for over an hour. She was forced down on the bed and choked to death, as indicated by the marks on her neck. Then, the killer stabbed her through the throat, for dramatic effect."

David Lemming stared at the chief. "What were you doing here?"

The chief looked flustered. "To be quite honest, I had a gut feeling about it when I remembered who she was. She was of course the suitemate of Virginia Kelly."

Lemming nodded. "Of course, I remember her. I even questioned her one day. A real interesting girl, she was. I'm sorry she's dead."

"Yes, she was a nurse at city general. Young girl. Too young to die."

Lemming chased away a fly from his face. "Was she raped?"

"No, it was the same as the other case. Whoever it was knew her, because there was no forced entry into the apartment, and not much struggle."

"If I recall, the first murder involved a lot of struggle," Lemming said.

"Or so it seemed."

Lemming studied the room with his observant eyes. "Any clues? Witnesses?"

Davis sat down and lit a cigarette. He took a couple of puffs and spoke.

"We found a glass downstairs. There was some fibers of clothing found on her fingers. I haven't questioned any neighbors yet."

"A glass?" Lemming spoke sharply, "What's so special about this glass?"

"Not much, except it looked like it was used lately."

"This girl was involved in the Kelly case and lived in the suite next to her," Lemming said reflectively, "isn't this a bit of a coincidence?"

"Possibly."

"Of course, it could be a copycat, like I said, or even a serial killer."

"Could be," Davis agreed. "Oh, another thing. They found an ounce of marijuana and a small sandwich bag of cocaine in her room."

Lemming brightened. "Is that right? Well, well, the parallels increase!"

Davis threw away his cigarette and lit another one. "We think we can find the drug supplier. I'm having her ex-roomie brought in for questioning."

"That Devereaux girl?" Lemming asked, shaking his head. "She's not involved."

Davis was surprised. "Why do you say that? She was her college roommate for three years. It stands to reason they would have the same supplier."

Lemming grinned. It was a condescending grin. "You're assuming Miss Sandy did drugs. She did not."

The chief blew a puff of smoke into the air and motioned for Lemming to sit down. "You better tell me what you know about the Kelly case."

Lemming sat down. "You know chief, those unfiltered cigarettes are really bad for you."

"Fuck the cigarettes," Davis's voice held tension, " How do you know anything about McKinley's roommate?"

"I don't know that much, chief. I did question McKinley and Devereaux after the Kelly murder. McKinley knew nothing, or so she said. Devereaux struck me as the type of girl who is more interested in shopping and sororities, if you know what I mean. She was the all American girl, not a druggie."

Davis stood up and paced. "I'm also going to question Kelly's ex-roomies. McKinley's boyfriend is also going to be questioned."

"She had a boyfriend?" Lemming asked sharply.

"Yes, a Robert Blackwood. Apparently the two had been having problems."

Lemming frowned. He had not counted on McKinley having a boyfriend. She did not seem to him to be the type to even have a boyfriend. He turned to leave.

"Keep me informed, chief."

Davis showed surprise. "What, you don't want to be involved in the questioning?"

"No. To be frank chief, I think you're barking up the wrong tree. This wasn't about drugs."

"No? How do you know this?"

Lemming smiled. "Intuition."

He left the room, leaving Davis to sit there and think.

53

Wednesday, April 18th, 1994

It was ten fifteen in the morning when Chief Davis and Detective Walker went into the questioning room the next day. As they entered the room, they noticed a man of medium built and exceptional good looks waiting for them. He rose to shake their hands.

"I'm detective Walker, and this is chief Davis," Walker said politely as the two sat down. The man was not nervous. In fact, he seemed happy.

"I'm Robert Blackwood, gentlemen. Nice to make your acquaintance."

Davis sized up Blackwood. A nice looking man. Broad shouldered, dark hair, fashionable clothes. He looked to be of Italian or eastern Mediterranean descent. Davis placed him to be around thirty years old.

"Mr. Blackwood, you do know why you are here?" he asked, lighting a cigarette.

"I assumed it was about the death of Traci yesterday," Blackwood said, waving his hands to fend away smoke. "Chief, do you mind? I don't care if you want lung cancer, but don't give it to me."

Davis was surprised at Blackwood's nerve. He said nothing though, and put out the cigarette.

"It was. But you don't seem too upset by it."

"Well shit happens, chief," Blackwood said casually. "It's not like I loved her. She's not the only girl I got."

A real charmer, Davis thought. "You have others?"

"Why sure!" Blackwood was enjoying himself, "I got two or three. Probably pick up another one today."

"Well, we're not here to discuss monogamy," Davis said. "Did you know about Miss McKinley's drug habits?"

"Sure. All you had to do is look at her to know she did drugs."

54

"Do you know the name of her supplier?"

Blackwood chuckled. "Now chief, you think she'd tell me? I don't do drugs, so why would she?"

"Very well. Are you familiar with Amy Sutherland, Colleen Duncan, or Sandy Devereaux?"

Blackwood chuckled again. "Did her, done her, doing her now."

Out of the corner of his eye, Davis saw Walker suppress a grin.

"Are you saying that you have had intimate relationships with all of these women?"

"What do you think?"

"Did you know Virginia Kelly?"

"Again, intimately," Blackwood was smiling from ear to ear. "Too bad she died too."

Davis sighed. "Well, you do get around, don't you Mr. Blackwood?"

"Don't hate me because I'm beautiful!"

Again, Davis noticed Walker suppress a grin.

"Well, do you have anything else to say other than you've slept with every woman in Denver?"

"Look chief," Blackwood began, "I won't pretend that I'm a saint. Yes, I cheated on Traci. Hell, it's what I do. I'm not a one-woman kind of man. I certainly did not kill either one of them though."

Davis looked into Blackwood's dark eyes. "It's certainly a coincidence you knew both these girls that were murdered."

Blackwood shook his head. "Not really chief. They all lived in the same building. I was dating Traci, so I knew all of them. Besides, why would I kill them? I'm Don Juan, chief, not Charles Manson."

"So you're seeing Miss Devereaux now?"

"Yes."

"How very Melrose Place, Mr. Blackwood."

"Touché."

"Mr. Blackwood, what is your occupation?"

"I mooch off women. They love to take care of me."

Walker spoke up. "Do you know of any reason that anyone would want Miss McKinley dead?"

Blackwood looked at Walker. "Not really. I thought it was a serial killer."

"Do you know anyone who drives a brown Toyota?" Walker continued.

"Brown Toyota? No, why?"

"Never mind," Davis broke in. "You can go now. Don't leave the city."

Blackwood got up. He spoke as if amused. "You mean I'm a dangerous suspect now?"

Davis looked up. "Possibly. Good day, Mr. Blackwood."

"Pleasure, gentlemen. Chief, you should really consider quitting that bad habit. And if you must smoke, change brands. Those really smell bad." Blackwood was smiling as he said this. He walked out, whistling happily.

Walker shook his head. "He's hard to read. Sounds like a typical womanizer, but I wonder if there's more to him?"

"A very dangerous guy," Davis observed.

Within two minutes, two girls were shown into the interview room. They were both in their mid to late twenties. Davis sized them up. The first one was a brunette, about five foot eight inches tall, pretty face, tan skin, and pale blue eyes. She was dressed casually, and did not seem very nervous at all. He looked at the second girl. She had light brown hair, cut shoulder length. She was not pretty, but had an appeal. She was about five-foot four, tan skin, and had large brown eyes. She was dressed in a business suit, so Davis judged her to be a professional woman.

"Good morning ladies, please have a seat," he said lightly.

The girls did so. The taller brunette spoke first.

"Can we ask why we were brought here? The cop who brought us in wouldn't answer us, except that it was real important."

Davis smiled and tried to look reassuring. "One thing at a time ladies. First let me introduce myself. I'm Chief Chandler Davis, and that man by the window is detective Walker. We just want to ask you a few questions about something that happened yesterday."

The girl did not share Davis's light mood. "I'm Amy Sutherland. She's Colleen Duncan. I guess since we were college roommates, this has something to do with that?"

Davis shifted his weight. "Perhaps. You girls remember a Traci McKinley?"

The two girls nodded.

"She was found stabbed to death yesterday in her apartment. Stabbed through the throat," Davis said, watching the girls' reactions carefully.

"Oh my God!" Amy Sutherland said, drawing in her breath.

Colleen Duncan's hands were on her mouth. She had turned pale.

"Are you okay ma'am?" Walker asked, coming forward.

Colleen held up her hand. "I'm okay."

"Chief Davis, one of our ex roommates was killed four years ago when we went to college," Amy said slowly.

Davis nodded. "Yes, I am aware of that. Her name was Virginia Kelly. This murder is very similar. That is why you two are here."

"But chief, you don't think we had anything to do with it?" Amy asked.

Davis looked down. "Miss Sutherland, the truth is, we have no idea who had anything to do with either murder. We think you can maybe shed some light."

Colleen spoke up. "But we were questioned in 1990. We really know nothing!"

"I found Virginia's body," Amy said, reflecting.

"Just a few questions," Davis said. "To begin with, what do you two do?"

"I'm a waitress right now at Ogura's Japanese Steak House," Amy said. "It's hard to find jobs these days."

"I'm a clerk at Gates Rubber," Colleen said.

"Do you two keep in touch with any of your college friends? Like maybe Sandy Devereaux?"

"I lost touch with Sandy, but I'm actually seeing a guy I knew back then," Amy said.

"Same here," Colleen said.

"Who would this guy be?" Davis leaned forward.

Amy was embarrassed. "Uh, I'd rather not say. It's kind of awkward now."

Colleen Duncan was a little surprised. "You too? To be

honest, chief, I'm the same way. My current boyfriend is someone who used to date Traci McKinley."

Davis raised an eyebrow. "Used to?"

Colleen shook her head. "Yes, he said he'd left her."

Amy Autherland turned to face her. "Wait a minute! Whom are you talking about?"

Davis had a picture of two girls flailing on the floor trying to pull each other's hair out in his head, so he broke in quickly. "That's not really important. What I need to know is do you have any reason to believe anyone you knew then would have any reason to harm Miss McKinley?"

Amy was still looking at Colleen suspiciously. "No, Traci was a quiet girl. I doubt if she had any enemies."

"I think she might have had an enemy. I remember she always talked about Virginia's murder like she almost knew what happened," Colleen said. "At times she was so sure of herself, I almost think she might have killed her. Of course, that's impossible, since she's been killed now."

Davis leaped on this. "Do you remember what she said exactly?"

Colleen thought for a moment. "She used to say that she was sure it wasn't a serial killer, and that even if she had heard anything that night, she wasn't stupid, and wouldn't tell police. She talked like she knew something."

"I see," Davis said, "And why does that make you think she had an enemy?"

"I'm not sure if it was an enemy," Colleen said, "but she did have strange phone calls after the murder. She'd often call someone on the phone and shut up or whisper if anyone came into her room. Me and Amy would sometimes come in to chat, and catch her at it."

"Strange phone calls? Was it a man? Woman?"

"I don't know. That's why I was a little suspicious of her. I thought that maybe she might be behind Virginia's murder, and was in cahoots with someone."

Amy Sutherland broke in. "Wait a minute! Do you think maybe she did? Maybe this person she was in cahoots with killer her!"

Davis stood up. "Miss Sutherland, that is a very astute

58

observation, but for your own safety, I suggest you keep that to yourself."

"Oh!" the girl was suddenly nervous.

"Another question," Davis continued. "Did you ever see Miss McKinley with any other man other than Robert Blackwood? Joe Thurman perhaps?"

"Joe?" Amy asked, and laughed. "No, Traci didn't really like Joe. I think she intimidated him."

"I did see a Latino guy with her sometimes. They were real buddy-buddy at parties, whenever Robert wasn't around," Colleen said.

"Oh yeah," Amy said, "That was Dan Martinez. He hung around with Virginia too. Drove a nice car."

"Who is Dan Martinez?" Davis asked sharply.

"I'm not sure," Amy said. "I vaguely remember Virginia telling me he was some hot shot. I personally think he was a drug dealer. He always wore a beeper, and he didn't look like a doctor."

"Walker, run a make on this Dan Martinez. Miss Sutherland, does the name Michael Barnard ring a bell?" Davis was pacing now.

"Barnard? Isn't that the name of that guy they arrested for Virginia's murder? I thought he was found innocent."

"He was acquitted," Davis said. "The reason I asked is that he was a known drug dealer. I'm wondering if his name ever came up with Miss Kelly or Miss McKinley."

Amy shook her head. "No, I even remember seeing his face in the papers. I had never seen him before."

Walker strode out to look up Dan Martinez. Davis lit a cigarette and eyed the two girls. "Do either one of you know anyone who drives a brown Toyota?"

The girls exchanged glances. They seemed to be thinking of an answer.

"Chief, I drive a brown Honda," Colleen said.

"I drive a blue Dodge, and I don't know anyone who drives a brown Toyota," Amy said flatly.

The chief nodded. "Very well ladies. That'll be all for now. You may go, but please don't leave town."

The girls got up and got their bags. They exchanged pleasantries and walked out of the room. Chief Davis stayed in the room for a minute. He had a lot of ideas in his head.

David Lemming stepped out into the street across from the hospital. As he walked towards the parking lot where his car was, he pondered on his next move. Should he visit Chief Davis again? He had just been inside talking to the pathologist who had done the autopsy on Traci McKinley. There were no surprises. The girl had died of strangulation, like he had known. She was later stabbed through the throat, which he had also known. He reached his car and got in. As he started it, a new idea came to him. He swung out of the parking lot and headed west.

There was a knock at the door. A middle-aged woman with dirty blond hair looked at it for a minute. She decided to open the door.

"Yes, what do you want?"

"Can I come in?" a voice sounded from outside the door.

The woman stepped aside. "Please do."

The owner of the voice outside stepped into the room slowly. Two legs walked over to the beat up chair in front of the television and sat down. Two eyes surveyed the room. The woman was not the cleanest person in the world.

"Nice place," the voice was sarcastic.

The woman snorted. "What do you want?"

Two eyes looked at her, and the person they belonged to, got up. A face was shoved two inches away from the woman's face. She smelled bad breath and turned her head away.

"I know you saw someone visit Miss McKinley yesterday around one o' clock. Do you know who that was?"

The voice had trailed away into a whisper.

The woman was trembling. "You know I do."

"What was he driving?"

"A silver Volvo."

"Did you get his license number?"

"I did. It was DSZ-443"

"Very good. And what did he look like?"

"Middle aged, pleasant looking man - brown hair. Wore a suit and tie. Looked very nervous."

"Could you identify him if you saw him again?"

"Yes."

A finger ran down the woman's right cheek. "Very good. You have a good memory."

The woman jerked her face away. "Look is there a reason..."

"Shhh..." she was cut off, "I needed confirmation. You're a witness now. And you're going to tell the police what you saw, aren't you?"

The woman nodded. The person in front of her turned and walked towards the door. As the door opened, the person looked at her again. A smile. A wicked smile.

"Relax, Mrs. Brown. No one can escape the truth."

A wink. The door was shut. The woman was left to herself. Breathing a sigh of relief, she went to the refrigerator to get a wine cooler. They helped calm her nerves.

Detective Walker came walking into the office of Chief Davis. His face held a look of excitement. Davis looked up from the paper he was reading.

"The lab report is in sir."

Davis looked at his watch. It was four thirty. "It's about time."

"The prints on the glass matched no known person in our criminal files, sir. But there were two different sets of prints. One was a bit blurred, but we still got it. The other was clear. It belongs to a man named Mark Kane."

"Mark Kane? Who's he?"

"He lives at 2114 Clayton drive, sir. No prior arrest record. I believe he's an engineer at KBATech."

Davis frowned. "And the other prints? They belong to the girl, I suppose."

"No sir. However, we're having trouble with it, it's very smudged."

Davis was a little puzzled. "Two prints huh? Well, work on that second print."

"Yes sir. Do you want Mark Kane brought in?"

"I'll bring him in myself," Davis said. "Did you run a make on Dan Martinez?"

"Yes sir," Walker said, "He's a known drug dealer. Has several arrest records, convicted once for dope dealing. Got two

61

years, served 8 months."

"Small time?"

"Not really, sir. He's suspected of being quite powerful, but it's hard to get any evidence on him."

Davis snorted in disgust. "It's the same story with all these sons of bitches. Put out an A.P.B on him, he may be our killer."

Walker left. Davis picked up the phone and dialed a number.

"Lemming Investigations."

"Mr. Lemming? Chandler Davis here. Looks like a break in our case. Interested?"

"Of course."

"The prints on the glass matched one Mark Kane. He's an engineer. No priors. There's another set of prints on the glass, but they are hard to decipher."

"I see."

"You want to go with me? I'm going to go pick Kane up."

"I'll be there in ten minutes."

Davis hung up. It was against his better judgment to call up Lemming, but he had a feeling that he could be some help. He did not like David Lemming, but he respected him professionally. He took out a piece of notebook paper and started jotting some ideas down.

Victims:
Virginia Kelly (1990), Traci McKinley (1994)
   - Both victims young college girls
   - Both murdered in same fashion, four years apart
   - Possible connection (serial killer) or copycat crime?
   - Possible planned murder?
Suspects:
1) Mark Kane - Professional Engineer, no record
   Motive - Unknown. Possible drugs?
   Evidence - Fingerprints on glass
2) Robert Blackwood - McKinley's boyfriend, 1 incident of
       public drunkenness in past. Ladies man, moocher.
   Motive: Desire for other woman? Get her out of way?
       Blackmail?

Evidence: None found yet
3) Sandy Devereaux - McKinley's ex-roommate, no record,
*   works in her dad's dentist's office.*
Motive: none known, possible jealousy?
Evidence: none known, yet to be interviewed.
4) Amy Sutherland, Colleen Duncan - McKinley's ex suitemates,
*   Kelly's ex-roommates, no record. Both employed.*
Motive: jealousy? money? drugs?
Evidence: none known
Intangibles: The other fingerprint on glass. Reports from
*   neighbors (not reviewed yet). Mysterious phone caller.*
*   Mystery man in brown Toyota. What was Mark Kane*
*   doing in McKinley's apartment?*

Chief Davis stopped writing, pondered, and then wrote down something else.

Possible darkhorse suspect: Joe Thurman?

The door opened and David Lemming walked in. He was smiling.

"Let's go chief."

Davis put on his jacket. The two strode outside. Lemming offered to drive. As the two pulled out onto the street, Lemming spoke.

"So this Kane fellow might be the drug supplier?"

"Maybe," Davis answered, "I'm also having a guy named Dan Martinez checked out. Kane looks like our man, though. His fingerprints are on the glass."

Lemming shook his head, still smiling.

"It's strange, though," Davis continued, "The guy is a professional engineer, works at a big company, and deals drugs to young women?"

"I've seen worse," Lemming stated. "I once unmasked a killer who was a priest. The man literally threw his life away because he was horny, but had to hide his sins."

"You'll have to tell me about it sometime," Davis said dryly.

Lemming guided his Chevy through a railroad crossing and

turned into a side road. They entered a nice subdivision in Glendale.

"Nice area," Davis commented.

Lemming nodded. "Yes, rich guys live here. Lawyers, doctors, businessmen..."

Davis looked at Lemming. "Why don't you live here? You should be a rich guy."

Lemming grinned. "Have you ever put your son or daughter through Harvard? It costs a few bucks."

"My son's graduated college already. He's an accountant in St. Louis."

"Where did he go?"

"University of Missouri. I don't have the big bucks like you," Davis said.

Lemming smiled again. "Well, my son's just a sophomore. He's going to be a lawyer. I'm proud of him, but it's damn expensive."

"Like father like son?"

Lemming frowned. "I'm not a lawyer."

"Both Harvard boys though, huh?"

"Yeah. But I didn't push him there. He wanted to go."

"Here we are," Lemming said, and turned into a driveway.

Mark Kane was washing his face. He had just finished shaving. It had been another long day at the office and he was looking forward to relaxing with his family. As he applied after-shave, the front doorbell rang. He looked up to see his daughter Trish run to the door. She opened it to reveal two men standing outside. They were both well dressed, and had serious looks on their faces. He thought he recognized one of them.

"Hi sweetheart," the taller of the two men said, "Is your daddy home?"

"Yes, he's in the bathroom," his daughter said, eyeing the two men with deep suspicion. Mark Kane walked out of the bathroom, toweling his face.

"I'm her daddy, gentlemen," he said with a smile. "What can I do for you?"

"Are you Mark Kane?" The taller man asked.

"Yes, that would be me," Kane said, his gaze shifting from

one man to the other.

"Mr. Kane, I'm chief Chandler Davis of Denver P.D.," the smaller man said, flashing a badge. "This is Mr. David Lemming, a private investigator. We need to ask you a few questions."

Kane's smile disappeared. He put down his towel. "Sure. Trish, go upstairs and get mommy."

The little girl ran upstairs. Chief Davis motioned for Kane to sit down. He did so. The two men continued to stand.

"Now Mr. Kane, are you aware of the murder of a young woman named Traci McKinley yesterday?"

Kane shook his head. "No, I'm not really up on my local news lately."

"Miss McKinley was twenty eight. She was a nurse at general," Davis said slowly, studying Kane's reaction.

"I'm sorry to hear that. What does this have to do with me?" Kane looked puzzled.

Becky Kane came down the stairs and stared at the two men. Chief Davis smiled at her.

"Honey, these are Chief Davis and Detective Lemming," Kane said, "They've come to ask me some questions. Have a seat."

Mrs. Kane sat down next to her husband. "Nice to meet you," she said uncertainly, "What's this all about?"

Davis sensed her unease. "Mrs. Kane, we're discussing the murder of Traci McKinley. Have you heard of it?"

"Oh yes, I heard about it on the news yesterday. Terrible thing," she said, and then looked at the two men skeptically. "But what does that have to do with us?"

Chief Davis looked grave. "Mr. Kane, there was a glass found at the house of the murdered woman. A freshly used glass. The glass contained some fingerprints," he paused for effect. "Your fingerprints."

Mark Kane looked at the chief like he was an alien from Mars. He opened his mouth, but said nothing. It was his wife who spoke.

"That's ridiculous, chief. There must be some mistake."

Davis shook his head. "No mistake ma'am. We did find some prints of Mr. Kane on record, and they match those on the glass."

Becky Kane looked at her husband. "You had fingerprints

on record?"

Kane nodded. "I had them put on record when I was a kid. Mom said it was a good way of tracking me down if I ever got lost."

"Mr. Kane, I'm going to have to arrest you for the murder of Traci McKinley. You have the right to remain silent. Anything you say can and will be used against you in a court of law. You have the right to an attorney. If you cannot afford one, one will be appointed for you. You have the right to a phone call. Do you understand these rights that I have informed you about?"

Kane nodded quietly as Davis put handcuffs on him. Becky Kane started shouting.

"This is crazy! Chief, Mark would never kill anyone!"

David Lemming had been quiet for a while. Now he looked at Mrs. Kane.

"Mrs. Kane, the evidence is all against your husband. We have reason to believe that your husband may have killed a woman as a result of perhaps a drug deal gone bad. Or maybe..." he looked her right in the eye," he was fooling around on you. Didn't want to pay the price. You know what I mean?"

"You son of a bitch!" Mrs. Kane hissed.

"That's enough," Davis shouted. "Let's go. Now!"

Mark Kane faced his wife calmly. "Becky, call Donna. Ask her to come by tomorrow. And call Phil Wellington. I think I'm going to need a lawyer."

He was taken out by Chief Davis and David Lemming, amid the protests of Rebecca Kane. When they were outside, Davis shot an angry look at Lemming.

"Was it necessary to say all that shit to her?"

Lemming smiled. "I wanted to watch her reaction. Call me an asshole if you like."

"You are an asshole, " Kane said quietly.

Lemming turned on him. "If I were you buddy, I wouldn't have that word in my vocabulary. They like pretty boys like you in prison."

Kane was calm. "You won't convict me."

"Shut up, both of you!" Davis said sharply, getting in the car. Kane was piled in, and they moved out. Kane looked over his shoulder through the rear window of Lemming's Chevrolet. His wife had run out to the street and was now looking at the car as it pulled away. The sky was dark grey against the western sun. Kane smiled to himself. He had a lot of confidence in her.

Thursday, April 19, 1994

It was early morning when Mark Kane was ushered out of his holding cell by a fat and kindly woman. He was met at the foot of the steps by Detective Matt Walker. He blinked as he came up to street level. It had been dark down in his cell, and his eyes had gotten accustomed to it.

"Your lawyer is here, along with your friend," Walker said. "They want to talk to you."

Kane was led into an office. He walked in and saw his old lawyer friend, Phil Wellington. He was pacing around. Donna Houseman was also there, sitting down in a comfortable looking chair. She was playing with a pencil. At the sight of Kane, Wellington stopped pacing and extended his had out to him.

"Mark, good to see you," he said. His voice was very serious.

Kane managed a smile. "You too Phil. Wish it was under happier circumstances."

Donna Houseman came over to hug him. Then she shoved him back and made an exasperated gesture with her hands.

"Mark, what the hell have you gotten yourself into?"

Kane sat down on top of a table. "I have no idea what's going on. All I know is that I have been arrested for murder. I seem to have murdered a girl that I've never even heard of. They found some fingerprints on some glass in her apartment. They turned out to be mine."

"Circumstantial," Wellington said.

"Forget that lawyer talk," Kane said. "It's impossible. I can't understand how this is happening."

"You think someone is trying to frame you?" Wellington askcd.

Kane shook his head. "I would say so. Either that or someone's made one huge mistake."

"Who in the world would want to frame you for murder,

Mark? Why?" Donna was incredulous.

Kane did not answer. Phil Wellington opened his briefcase and got out a notepad and pen. He looked up at Kane.

"Listen, your bail hearing is tomorrow. We have to get them to allow bail, so we can investigate and figure out what the hell is going on. Now, the murder occurred sometime around 1:30 on Tuesday. Do you have an alibi for that time?"

Kane's face clouded. He had a knot in his stomach. As he spoke, his words came out slowly.

"Thuesday at 1:30 I was eating lunch at Branson's."

"Good!" Wellington brightened," Who were you eating with? All we have to do..."

He was cut off by Kane. "I was by myself."

Wellington was surprised. Donna was shocked.

"Mark, you never eat alone," she said.

"I know," Kane began to explain, "Nate Goodson called me and asked me to meet him there for lunch. We were going to discuss the 067 part."

"So what happened?"

Kane shrugged. "He never showed up."

Wellington dropped his pen. "Did you ask him why he stood you up?"

"No, never got around to it. Guess something came up."

"Is that typical with him?"

"No, Nate's usually quite reliable."

Donna got up and began pacing. She suddenly stopped and stared at Kane. She had an idea.

"Mark, you're sure it was Nate who called you?"

"Yes, I am..." Kane began. "At least it sounded like him. I think..."

"But are you sure?"

Kane thought furiously. "Let's see... It was about 11:20 or so, my phone rang, and he greeted me. I didn't really pay attention to make sure it was him. He then immediately asked me to join him at Branson's for lunch. I assumed he wanted to discuss the part, because we had missed lunch the day before, and..."

Donna broke in. "...You assumed?"

Kane sighed. "I'm not sure. I guess it could have been someone else. I really didn't notice, nor was I looking to notice.

69

When your phone rings you really don't..."

Donna cut him off again. "Rings? Did you say rings?"

Kane frowned. "Uh yes, I..."

"But Mark, our office phones don't ring on an internal intercom to intercom call! They beep! Only call from outside lines ring! And I know for a fact that Nate Goodson was inside the plant around 11:20."

Wellington whistled. "So someone from an outside phone called you to meet at Branson's at 1:30, impersonating Nate. Perhaps this person was setting you up to not have an alibi at that time, buddy."

Kane was thunderstruck. Donna was right, internal calls beeped, they did not ring. And that phone had definitely rung. Why hadn't he thought of it? Then he thought of something that made his heart sink even lower.

"Guys, I have no alibi. Phil, you're right, no one saw me at Branson's!" he said frantically. "No one even saw me leave from work!"

"What about the waiter?" Wellington asked.

"I never go there. He'd never remember me. Hell, I don't even remember what he looked like."

"This is really too convenient for the murderer," Donna stated. "We can't let him get away with this."

Kane gave her hand a small squeeze. "Thanks guys, for believing me."

Donna made a face. "Like we'd believe you're capable of murder, Mark. You forget how long I've known you."

Wellington patted Kane on the back. "That's right. We'll get you out of this. I'll get in touch with this Nate fellow, and ask him if he called. Now remember, don't say a thing to Chief Davis unless I am present. They can't make you answer any questions."

Kane nodded. "Don't worry, I've already told him that questioning me would do no good, I'd take the fifth on everything."

Donna and Phil got ready to go. As they were walking out, Kane called out.

"Donna!"

She turned to face him.

"How's Becky and the kids holding up?"

"They're okay," she said. "Becky even went to work today.

Don't worry, they're behind you all the way. You'll see them tomorrow when I post bail and get you out of here."

Kane smiled meekly. "If bail is allowed."

"It will be," Donna said, with a confident smile. "Keep your chin up."

The two walked out. Kane lowered his gaze. A spider was walking across the table. He went to crush it with his hand, but something made him stop. He smiled to himself. He saw himself in the spider. Yes indeed, they were both at the mercy of a higher power, and at the moment, he didn't feel like playing God and taking the life of the insect.

Detective Walker came in and walked him back to his cell. He was still thinking of the spider as they walked. He had always hated spiders, but now they had a special meaning. A meaning only he would understand.

Friday, April 20, 1994

As Mark Kane entered the courtroom the next day for his hearing, he noticed that the courtroom was full of people. He did not want this. The mugging he received from the press just outside the hall was enough to make him nauseous, and now this. He looked around the many faces that were now staring at him as he walked up to the front of the courtroom. These were not friendly faces. Who knew that a bail hearing could attract so much attention?

Phil Wellington was walking right beside him. He leaned over to him and whispered, "They're ready to feed me to the wolves."

"Don't worry, they have no influence over a judge's decision, " Phil whispered back.

The men sat down. Kane took a quick look behind him, being careful not to catch anyone's eye. Becky was there, and she smiled at him reassuringly. The kids were not there, but they were in school. School did not excuse you if your dad was in trouble with the law. He looked over at the prosecutor. She was a tall, dark haired woman of about forty years of age. Her eyes met his. She gave him a polite smile. He did not smile back.

"That's Kim Randall, otherwise known as the terminator," Wellington explained.

"Wonderful," Kane retorted.

The bailiff stood up. His deep throaty voice echoed across the room.

"Hear-ye, hear-ye. This hearing is in session. All rise!"

The all got up. Out of the corner of his eye, Kane spotted Donna in the back of the room. She did not look nervous at all. He was glad to see that, because he did not feel very confident at all.

The judge strode in. He was a heavyset black man. He looked to be in his fifties. He was bald, and he did not look like he was in a good mood. Did a judge ever look happy, Kane thought to himself.

72

"The honorable Lawrence Daniels presiding," the bailiff finished.

Judge Daniels sat down and made a motion with his hand. "You may sit. Let us be quick this morning, ladies and gentlemen. I not only have a toothache, but I have a very busy agenda this morning."

The crowd sat down. Kim Randall immediately got back up. "That will not be a problem your honor. This is an open and shut case."

"Get on with it."

"Your honor, the first case is The State of Colorado versus Mark Kane. The case against this defendant is very strong. We will show you that we have proof of his guilt. He was at the house of the victim, Traci McKinley, at the night of the murder."

"Objection your honor...," Wellington jumped in.

"Mr. Wellington, this is not a trial. Let Mrs. Randall speak."

"Miss."

Daniels frowned. "Excuse me?"

"Miss Randall," Randall said, "You called me Mrs. Randall."

Judge Daniels put down his papers and looked straight at Kim Randall. "Thank you for letting us in on your marital status, MISS Randall. In the future, do not correct me in my courtroom. Do we understand each other?" His tone was as sharp as a razor.

"Yes, your honor," Randall did not sound intimidated.

"Good," Daniels said. "Now let us continue."

"Your honor, as you can see in the police file in front of you, the fingerprints of a glass found at the scene of the crime matched those of Mr. Kane's. We also found traces of lint on the woman's clothes that were distinctly different from her clothing. They turn out to match a flannel shirt of the defendant's."

"Your honor, many people own flannel shirts exactly like the one Mr. Kane owns," Wellington spoke up, "This is the nineties, flannel is in."

"Your honor, the prosecution can also prove that during the time of one to two o 'clock Tuesday afternoon, Mark Kane's whereabouts are unknown to all but one person," Randall continued. "This person is an eyewitness who saw Mr. Kane drive up to the defendant's apartment at approximately the time of the murder. This person saw him come into the apartment, and leave about ten minutes later."

Kane looked at Wellington in surprise. Wellington looked like he had also been totally taken by surprise. This was obviously news to him.

"Your honor," Wellington said, composing himself, "We have no knowledge of any such eyewitness."

Daniels looked at him. "Well now you do. Miss Randall, go on."

Wellington sat down in disgust. Randall went on. "Your honor, in lieu of this evidence, we ask that bail be denied and that a trial by jury for first degree murder be the only choice."

Wellington got up quickly. "Your honor, what Miss Randall calls evidence, I call hear say. My client has no prior record. He did not commit this crime. He feels that he is being framed. He is a highly respected professional individual. He is also a loving husband and the father of two children. We ask that bail be granted, and that it be minimal."

Randall looked at Wellington with an amused look on her face. She worded with her lips. "Minimal?"

Judge Daniels hesitated a moment and looked at the well-dressed Mark Kane. He looked every bit the respectable man. He came to a decision.

"There is certainly ample evidence here for a trial. However, in review of Mr. Kane's lack of a police record and his standing in the community, I will allow bail. Bail is set at five hundred thousand dollars. The trial will be set for July fourteenth. Jury selection will begin next Tuesday." He banged down his gavel. "Next!"

The crowd started to disperse, and Wellington looked over at Kane. Kane was looking relieved. "Well, at least I can get out there and try to find the real killer."

Becky came down and put her arms around him. Donna also made her way down.

"We'll make bail immediately," Donna said.

Kane nodded his head. "I won't let you all down."

"We're going to have to hire a detective. I know a good one downtown," Wellington said.

Donna brushed him off with a wave of her hand. "A detective? He can't afford one after he gets through paying you. I'll be his detective."

Kane laughed. "Donna, you don't know the first thing about being a detective!"

She winked. "Trust me."

"Let's go," Wellington said. The four went out the door and headed for the outside entrance. A man was running toward them. It was David Lemming.

"What do you want?" Kane asked sharply.

Lemming grinned and drew back in mock horror. "Such hostility! Listen Kane, you screwed up."

"I didn't do it."

"That's the most popular phrase of all accused felons."

"In this case, it's true," Kane said.

"Someone saw you, Kane."

"She's lying."

Lemming's smile became crooked. "Who told you it was a she?"

Wellington broke in. "Listen, Mr. Lemming. My client is not going to talk to anyone. He is innocent until proven guilty."

"You lawyers love delaying the inevitable, don't you?" Lemming asked. "Milk your client for all his money and then leave him to rot."

Wellington did not answer. Lemming started to walk off.

"Mr. Lemming, if you do some detecting, you'll find I didn't do it," Kane called out.

Lemming looked back. "Mr. Kane, the detecting has just begun."

He strode off. Kane stared at him. "I don't like that man."

"He's got a way about him," Wellington said. "Irritating as hell. His record is incredible, though. Wish he was on our side."

Donna opened the door and was immediately mobbed by a team of reporters. There were microphones shoved in Kane's face. Everyone was firing questions.

"Mr. Kane, were you involved in two murders?"

"Mr. Kane, was Miss McKinley a hooker?"

"Listen!" Wellington yelled. "My client has nothing to say. Please allow us to get to the car."

75

The group waded through the mob and stumbled into the waiting car, all along being peppered with questions. Kane felt as if he was in a daze. As they were safely inside the car, he spoke.

"God, I'm a celebrity now."

"Yes," Wellington said, sighing. "This is probably one of the biggest murder cases Denver has seen in a while. Add to it the possibility of a serial killer, and it's a sure fire hit tv movie of the week."

Kane managed a smile. "Maybe I ought to write a book."

Becky Kane had remained quiet throughout the ordeal. Now she faced her husband. "What was all that about an eyewitness?"

Mark Kane's face was grim. "I don't know. It doesn't make any sense to me."

"Mark, if an eyewitness says he saw you, you're as good as hanged!" She started to cry. Kane put his arms around her as she wept quietly. He felt sorry for her. He really felt sorry that she and the kids were being put through all this. A trickle of guilt crept up at him. Wellington broke the silence.

"Now listen Becky, all is not lost. We have some time on our hands. We'll find the real killer."

Becky said nothing. Mark Kane looked out the car window. The day had turned into a nice one. The sun was out. It was a good day to be alive, he thought; even if one was charged with murder, life was still worth living.

☠

Saturday, April 21, 1994

"...An engineer at KBAtech, a large manufacturing company in the Denver suburbs. Kane works as an engineer there, and is described as a likable and friendly person by his colleagues. That is what makes it so bizarre that..."

A hand reached across the TV set and turned down the volume.

"It's funny," Frank McKinley said to his wife, "I figured that asshole Blackwood did it."

Lynne McKinley sat on the couch and stared vacantly. She said nothing, and there were tearstains on her face. Her husband sat down on the lazy boy next to her and looked at a potted plant on the side table. He didn't feel like talking much either. Ever since his daughter Traci had been killed, his wife had not said a word. She had just gone about her business. She hadn't even cried that much. It was this morning that she had finally broken down and cried. Let her, he thought. She needs to get it out. He felt sorry for her, even though they had been having problems as a couple lately. With Lynne, it was always something. Lately, if he said black, she would say white. After thirty-two years of marriage, things were dwindling. It was tragic that a thing like the death of their daughter would bring them closer together again.

Frank McKinley got up and drew back the curtains to reveal a gorgeous blue Tennessee sky. They had been living in Knoxville for the last seventeen years. Now that he had retired, he was going to settle here. He looked at the Kyle boy racing by on his bicycle and sighed. He couldn't even look at someone young without thinking of his daughter. Why couldn't Traci have stayed home and gone to the University of Tennessee? She had to go all the way to Colorado. Not that she had done badly. She had turned out to be a good nurse. The Blackwood boy's face floated into his mind. His face tightened. The scoundrel! He slept around on Traci, he had no doubt of that. He probably murdered his sweet daughter and framed this poor person on TV.

He squinted as he saw a white Ford pull into his driveway. He wasn't expecting a visitor. The car parked and an attractive woman stepped out. She was wearing a sweatshirt, as it was slightly cool this morning in the Tennessee hills. He saw her come up to the door and ring the bell.

"I'll get it," he called out and answered the door. The woman smiled at him and extended her hand. She was not wearing a ring.

"Mr. McKinley? My name is Donna Houseman. May I talk to you a minute?"

"Talk? I'm not buying anything," McKinley said, hoping to convey that he wasn't in a talkative mood.

"No sir, I'm not selling anything," the woman said, smiling. "I'm an investigator. I'm looking into the death of your daughter, Traci. Let me first convey to you my deepest condolences, it was a tragedy."

McKinley stepped aside to let her in. She came in and looked around.

"Nice house."

"Thank you," McKinley said gruffly. "Come on into the living room."

Donna walked into the room and looked around some more. A woman sat on the couch and looked at her as if she wasn't even there. She seemed to look older than she actually was. Donna wondered how a person could look that way.

"Have a seat," McKinley said. "This is my wife, Lynne."

She sat down and smiled at Lynne McKinley. "Hello."

She did not seem to hear her.

"Don't mind her, she's still in some shock," McKinley sounded apologetic.

"I understand."

"Now," McKinley said, leaning back in his seat, "What brings you here?"

Donna took a deep breath. "Well, Mr. McKinley, let me first start by saying that I am not actually a detective. My reasons for coming here are selfish reasons. I want to free the man accused of murdering your daughter. I do not believe he did it, and I am here to seek some answers to questions that I have."

McKinley was silent for a moment. "So you don't think Mr. Kane is guilty." He did not phrase the words as a question, but as a statement. Donna shook her head.

"No, I do not. To be perfectly honest, I know he didn't do it."

McKinley was interested. "No? How do you figure?"

Donna hesitated before answering. "I know Mark Kane. He is not capable of cold blooded murder."

"Maybe it was the heat of the moment."

"I don't think he would commit murder, even on the heat of the moment. Plus, I don't think he knew your daughter."

"You're a good friend to come all the way here for him."

"I'd go all the way around the world if necessary."

McKinley rose. "Do you want a drink? Maybe a coke?"

"No thank you."

He strode off to the kitchen and grabbed a can of coke out of the fridge.

"Who do you think did it then, Miss Houseman?"

"I wish I knew."

He came back and sat down. Fishing in his pocket, he got out a penny to pry his can open. He laughed. "These things are always so tight."

Donna smiled. "Mr. McKinley, can we get down to business?"

"Of course," he said, taking a sip of his coke. "Fire away."

"Okay," Donna began, "First of all, tell me a little about your daughter."

McKinley reflected. A nostalgic smile came to his face. "Well, Traci was always different. Even when she was a little girl, she marched to a different drum. I remember on her fifth birthday, she asked for world peace as a present."

He looked at Donna. "Can you imagine? Not a Barbi Doll or a toy kitchen set or a pony. World peace."

Houseman waited silently for him to continue. He did.

"Anyway, what can I say? Traci was always an intelligent girl. In high school she got almost straight A's. She wasn't your typical teenager. She didn't have any boyfriends. She didn't date. It was her junior year that she decided that she would go to Colorado for her college education. I guess she just wanted a change of

79

scenery. She got a full scholarship. She graduated in '91 and immediately got a job."

"At Denver General?"

"Yes."

"Did she have many boyfriends in college?"

Frank McKinley sighed. "One after another. Her hormones kicked in as soon as she got to college. She outgrew them and settled on a guy named Robert Blackwood."

Donna shifted in her chair. "You know Mr. Blackwood well?"

"Only saw him during Christmas. That was last December."

"How was their relationship?"

"That's just it. I never thought their relationship was anything more than platonic. They never seemed very close when they were here."

"Yet they were set to be married?"

"This July. Traci told me that she needed the stability in her life."

"Mr. Blackwood is an attractive man?"

"I suppose so. He's one of these guys who live at the gym. Fairly smart guy, and the body of a Greek God. He was popular with women."

"Weren't you surprised that your daughter would consider marrying him?"

McKinley nodded. "I was more than surprised. Traci was always very cerebral. She always went on about how a man would never use her. She always hated macho assholes. Next thing you know, she's engaged to one."

Donna was taking notes on a pad. She now put her pencil down and motioned towards Lynne McKinley. "How did she feel about him?"

"I can talk, dear," Lynne McKinley said in a clear voice. Her eyes were shining brightly.

"Of course, " Donna was apologetic. "Mrs. McKinley, what was your opinion of Robert Blackwood?"

"I'll tell you something," she answered. "Robert is a lot of things. He's vain, egotistical, and arrogant. He played around. He was not, however, smart enough for Traci. Traci could read him like a book."

Donna was interested. "What are you trying to say?"

"I'm saying that he couldn't plan her murder without giving it away to her. She'd see him coming a mile away."

"You're assuming it was a planned murder?"

"Of course it was. Someone had planned it for months, maybe years. Let me give you a piece of advice. If you want your killer, look for a cold, calculating type, not a hot blooded type."

"Could it have been a woman, Mrs. McKinley?" Donna asked intently.

Lynne McKinley looked up at the ceiling. She was not going to say any more. He husband whistled. "Well, that's the most she's talked since Traci's death."

Donna pressed on. "Did you know Virginia Kelly?"

"Yes of course, I knew Virginia and Sandy quite well. You know, Virginia was killed in 1990," McKinley said, with a look of sadness. "She was killed in the same manner as..."

He fell silent. Donna seized the opportunity.

"Can you tell me something about..."

McKinley broke in. "Forget them. You need to talk to someone else."

He got up to go to his desk, sitting adjacent to the side window. He went through his drawers. Soon, he pulled out a small book. He walked back to Donna and handed it to her. It was an address book.

"You need to go see Luisa Gutierrez. She lives right here in Knoxville."

Donna read the address beside the name: Luisa Gutierrez - 1830 Gleason road. She looked up quizzically.

"Who is she?"

"She's the only real friend Traci's ever had. She could tell you things about her that I could not. They also roomed together at Colorado their freshman year."

"All right, I think I'll pay her a visit," Donna said, getting up. She wrote down her phone number on a sheet of paper and handed it to the old man. "Please call me if you think of anything."

"I will," he said, showing her to the door. She started to walk out. He put his hand on her shoulder, catching her by surprise.

"By the way, good luck. I don't think your friend did it

either."

Donna smiled and went out, her faith in humanity somewhat revived.

A few minutes later, Donna was at a gas station payphone, dialing a number. The phone rang twice, and was picked up.

"Hello." It was a man's voice. He spoke with a slight Latino accent.

"Hi, could I speak with Miss Luisa Gutierrez please?"

"She's not here."

"I see. Could you have her call me back please? When she gets back?"

"Okay."

"My name's Donna Houseman. Have her call me at the downtown Hilton. The number's 555-6917. I'm in room 614."

"I'll do it."

"Have her leave a message if I'm not there! It's very important!"

She hung up, hoping that the man wouldn't forget. She wasn't sure of her next move, so she dialed another number, and placed a collect call. A minute later, she was talking to Mark Kane.

"Donna, how's it going down there?"

She filled him in on the situation and asked about proceedings in Denver.

"Things are moving," Kane answered. "Phil's already tracked down this mysterious witness, and he'll talk to her tomorrow. A lawyer named Donald Watts called me and wants to talk to me. Seems he's interested in my case."

"Donald Watts? Wasn't he involved in that Kelly case?"

"Uh-huh. Seems he tried to prosecute some guy for that who got away because of lack of evidence. He is very interested in Traci McKinley's murder, because the M.O. was similar."

Donna bit her lip. "Have the police talked to this witness? Who is she?"

"Some woman who lived next door to the murdered girl. Her name is Teresa Brown," Kane explained. "Listen to this though; another neighbor of McKinley's, Pat Layman, says he saw some guy in a brown Toyota take a potshot at McKinley earlier on the day she was murdered. McKinley had complained to Davis

82

about the mysterious Toyota, as well."

Donna's grip on her receiver tightened. "Are you serious? How did you find out?"

"Chief Davis called me and let me know. The guy's okay, you know. I don't think that he truly believes that I did it."

"That's encouraging," Donna said. "We really need to check out this Toyota lead, whoever was driving it is our man."

"I know. Phil's doing some legwork while you're away. I'm bored, I wish I could help," Kane said in a disconsolate voice.

Donna looked at her watch. "Listen Mark, say hi to Becky and the kids for me. I'm going to talk to Luisa Gutierrez later today. I'll be back tomorrow."

"Okay. You be careful!"

She hung up the phone and pondered her next move. Her stomach rumbled. She realized what her next move would be. It was lunchtime.

Chief Chandler Davis pressed the doorbell of apartment two. It was the Deerfield lane apartments. He had called Teresa Brown earlier and scheduled a meeting. He was somewhat angry with Kim Randall for not letting him in on this witness.

The door opened and he was looking into the eyes of a plump middle-aged woman. She had a pleasant face. Her hair was dirty blond, and she had nervous blue eyes. Davis sized her up. She looked to be about forty, was probably divorced, and probably hated men. She was probably an Oprah watcher. It was a habit of his to speculate about people's personalities before he knew the facts. Too often he was right. Now he smiled at the middle-aged lady, and she smiled back. It was a nervous smile.

"Miss Brown, I'm Chief Davis. I called you earlier."

"Oh yes, come in," she said, opening the door wider.

Davis stepped into the apartment. Miss Brown was not the neatest person in the world. There were pizza boxes and remains of fast food packages everywhere. Clothes were piled up on top of the couch. Beer bottles with cigarette butts sticking out of them lay about.

"Did you have a party recently?" he asked.

"Sorry about the mess," Teresa Brown said meekly, "I haven't had much time to clean lately. I'm working nightshift, and

I'm always tired."

Davis sat down on a wooden chair and faced the nervous woman. He put on his most serious face.

"Miss Brown, let me cut to the chase. You called Kim Randall and told her that you had witnessed someone come into Miss McKinley's apartment at the time of her murder?"

The woman's head nodded vigorously.

"You say you saw a silver Volvo park outside, and a middle aged, brown haired man in a suit walk into her apartment?"

"Yes."

"Why were you watching her apartment at the time?"

"I was outside, sweeping my walk."

"I see. Did this man see you?"

"He didn't really look at me."

"And you're sure of the time?"

"Yes. I always eat lunch at one. I finished, and went outside to sweep. It was around one thirty."

Davis cleared his throat. "Have you seen a picture of Mr. Mark Kane?"

"Yes, Miss Randall showed me one. It was him all right."

"Did you see any other people visit Miss McKinley that day?"

"Just her boyfriend."

"What! When was this?" Davis spoke sharply.

"It was earlier, around ten or so."

"I didn't really know him, but he had said hello to me once or twice. I think his name's Robert. A very good looking guy," Teresa Brown said, blushing a little.

"Miss Brown, are you married?"

"Divorced two years. I have a child, but he's with his dad."

"Where do they live?"

"Kansas City. The court decided that he should be with Gary, because he is a doctor, and makes money. I guess he offers more stability than I do."

"What do you do, Miss brown?"

Teresa Brown sighed. "I work third shift at Gates. It pays the bills."

"Aren't these apartments pretty expensive?" Davis asked, looking around.

The woman flushed. "Well, they're not too bad. I like to live nice."

"I see you have a new car," Davis said, parting back the curtains and looking outside. "I am assuming that new Mustang GT is yours."

She flushed again. "Yes, it's mine. I bought it a week ago."

Davis got up. "Don't those cost over twenty grand? Gates must be paying quite a lot to its production workers these days." He was smiling.

"Well, yes, but my husband pays me ali..."

"Miss Brown, why did you get divorced?" Davis broke in sharply.

Teresa Brown hesitated a moment, and then regained her composure. "Well chief Davis, I really don't think that..."

"Was it because you cheated on your husband?"

"Well, I..."

"Doesn't speak well for your character does it?"

"Look, chief, this is really none of your business!"

Davis frowned. "Never mind, I can find out all I need to know about you," he said sharply. He walked towards the door. "Meanwhile, I'd advise you to stay in town. And keep this in mind: Lying in court is perjury, and is punishable by jail time."

Teresa Brown stared open mouthed as chief Davis left, slamming the door behind him.

It was almost five thirty when Donna Houseman got back to her hotel. She ran into the lobby and practically shoved an old lady aside to get to the counter. A traffic jam on the interstate had made her late.

"Any messages for Donna Houseman, room 614?" she asked breathlessly.

The short bald man at the desk gave her a polite smile and checked a file.

"No, none."

She rushed past the surprised faces and pressed the elevator button. In what seemed to her to be hours, but was actually thirty seconds, the door opened and she jumped inside. As soon as she reached her floor, she raced out and headed for her room. She thought she could hear the phone ringing. She fumbled with her keys and dropped them on the floor.

"Damn!"

She finally found her key and got the door opened. She rushed in and ran the phone down. It was still ringing, to her amazement.

"Hello!" she shouted.

"Miss Donna Houseman?" The voice was female.

"Yes, that's me."

"This is Luisa Gutierrez. My brother told me that you had called earlier."

"Yes, I did. Miss Gutierrez..."

"Call me Luisa."

"Uh, Luisa, you are friends with a Traci McKinley?"

Luisa's voice died down. "Yes."

"Are you aware that..."

"Yes, I have heard. I'm attending the funeral Saturday." Her voice was somewhat cold.

"Luisa, I need to talk to you. I'm representing Mr. Mark Kane, he's been..."

"He's been charged with her murder. Why would I want to talk to you if you represent him?"

Cold as steel.

"Luisa, please let me finish," Donna said, "We have very good reason to believe he didn't do it. You want to find the real killer, don't you?"

Luisa was silent for a moment. Then she said in a slow, deliberate voice, "I am not really interested, Miss Houseman."

"But..."

"Sorry. Have a good evening."

She hung up. Donna stared at her receiver. This was not what she had expected of Luisa Gutierrez. She hung the phone up slowly and sat down on the bed. What would she do now? A map of Knoxville lay on the nightstand. She looked at it and made up her mind. She grabbed the map and opened it. It took her a minute to find Gleason road on the map. It looked to be about eight miles from downtown. She could make that in fifteen or twenty minutes, she estimated. She grabbed her key and ran out of her room. She stopped at the front desk downstairs. The bald man looked up at her with the same smile as before. She didn't like this man.

"Listen, if anyone calls for me, please take down their name and number. It's very important."

"We always do, ma'am."

She turned and strode away.

About fifteen minutes later, Donna had found 1830 Gleason road. The area was nice, and was full of large houses with half-acre lots. Large trees gave the neighborhood a very "vanilla" flavor, but this was to Donna's liking. She pulled her rental car into the driveway of a two-story foyer. There was a white Lexus parked outside. She walked right up to the door and rang the bell. It was opened by a little olive complexioned girl. She didn't seem to be over four years old.

"Hi!" Donna said with a smile. "Is Luisa home?"

"Mommy's taking a shower," the girl said with a big grin on her face.

"Well, do you mind if I come in and wait for her?"

The girl looked suspicious. "Mommy said I shouldn't let strangers in."

Donna smiled and nodded. "You know what, your mommy's right. I'll wait for her out here."

The girl seemed hesitant. "But it's a little cold out here."

"That's okay," Donna said. "My name's Donna. What's yours?"

The girl giggled. "I'm Anna. I think you're a nice lady. You can come in."

"Well, thank you sweetie," Donna said and walked in.

The house was a fairly large one. She stepped up a half flight of stairs to the living room, followed by Anna. As she sat down, she noticed a picture of the little girl on the wall. With her was a very beautiful Latino woman and a handsome blond haired man. This must be Luisa, she thought, and the man must be her husband. Luisa had pretty black hair and large black eyes. She looked somewhat like a Spanish queen.

"Are you looking at Mommy's picture?" Anna asked and sat down next to her.

"Yes I am," Donna said. "Your mommy's pretty."

"As pretty as me?"

"No, you're prettier."

This comment seemed to please the little girl very much, as she broke into a huge grin. Donna looked at her wistfully and wondered what it would be like to have a little boy or girl of her own. At that moment, Luisa walked into the room, wearing a black robe and toweling her hair dry.

"Who is it Anna? What..."

Donna rose from her chair and extended her hand. "Hi Mrs. Gutierrez, I'm Donna Houseman."

"Isn't she pretty, mommy?" Anna asked, giggling.

Luisa was not laughing. "Anna, go to your room."

"But mommy..."

"Go to your room hija!"

Anna left sullenly. Luisa put her towel away and looked at Donna malevolently. She was not at all pleased to have a total stranger in her house.

"I thought I told you I wasn't interested."

Donna came forward. "Look, Mrs. Gutierrez ... "

"Call me Luisa."

"Luisa, please don't be like that. I am quite sure that you are grief stricken by Miss McKinley's death, but..."

"Who told you so?" Luisa interrupted again. Donna had the feeling she did that a lot.

"Well, naturally I assumed..."

"You shouldn't assume anything," Luisa said sharply and sat down. "Have a seat."

Good, Donna thought. She's going to talk. Her gamble had paid off.

"Wasn't she your best friend in high school and college?" she asked, sitting down in a chair.

Luisa crossed her legs. "I suppose she was, till my freshman year in college."

"What happened then?"

Luisa bit her lip. "Look, I really don't think I want to talk to some P.I. about this."

"I'm not a P.I. I'm just a good friend of the man who's been accused of her murder."

Luisa was surprised. "You really must think he's innocent, then?"

"I'm sure of it. That's why I am here. I desperately need

some answers."

Luisa stared out the window for a minute. She seemed to be making a decision. Finally she spoke.

"All right. I'll answer your questions."

Donna brightened and took out her notepad. "Good. Now, what happened in college to strain your relationship with Traci?"

Luisa stared straight ahead. "To put it bluntly, she stole my boyfriend."

"I see. And this happened when?"

"1988. We were very close. Then I walk in early one day because History class has been cancelled. Guess who I catch frolicking on the couch?"

"Your boyfriend and Traci?"

"Right. Anyway, later I found out that he was sleeping with other girls, so the pain was easier to take. What was done was done, though. Traci had stabbed me in the back."

"So you harbor some resentment toward her?" Donna asked, writing furiously.

Luisa reflected. "No, I felt sad. I knew that he'd cheat on her too, and I'm sure he did. Anyway, after our freshman year we went our separate ways and I didn't stay in touch with her."

"Did you by chance know Virginia Kelly?"

"No, who's she?"

"She was murdered in 1990 in the same manner as Traci was. She was a suitemate of hers for a while."

Luisa frowned. "Ay Madre, that's interesting!"

Donna nodded. "Isn't it? I'm surprised that you've never heard of her."

"Like I said, we lost touch," Luisa said, playing with her hair, "although I do remember a murder vaguely. I'm not good with names."

Donna changed the subject. "So Luisa, when did you get married?"

"Married? I'm not married. Bill and I live together."

"Oh! So Anna is yours and his child?"

Luisa shook her head. "No, no. She's Robert's child."

Donna sat up straight and stared at her. "Robert?"

"Robert Blackwood. The boyfriend I was talking about."

"Well, well, the plot thickens," Donna said under her

breath.

"Excuse me?"

"Nothing. So Anna is how old?"

"She's five and a half. I know she looks younger. Bill cares for her like his own daughter."

"Another question. Were you aware of Traci's drug problem?"

Luisa lowered her eyes. "I'd say I was. I had the same problem."

Donna leaned forward. "Who was your supplier?"

"Well, I might as well tell you. I don't do the stuff anymore. His name was Dan Martinez. He was a two-bit piece of shit, but he always had the goods. He made his female customers do sexual favors for him if they didn't have the money. Luckily Traci always had the money."

"She was rich?"

"Yes, although I could never figure out how. Her parents were middle class people. She didn't earn much. Yet she always had plenty of money."

"Maybe she was selling?" Donna pressed.

Luisa licked her lips. "No, I doubt it. I would have known."

"Did you know her roommates after your parting of ways?"

"Her roommate Sandy was in a few of my classes. She wasn't my type."

"One last question. Did anything about ever Traci strike you as strange?"

Luisa thought for a minute. "Yes. She started having strange phone conversations with someone midway through our freshman year. It was like she was negotiating with someone over the phone. I could never figure it out, and she wouldn't ever tell me what it was about."

Donna thought for a moment. Was Traci McKinley blackmailing someone? Whom? A professor? Blackwood? A fellow student? Was she being blackmailed herself? How was she getting money? She had no answers. She was getting vague clues, and it was like trying to put together a jigsaw puzzle. She came to a conclusion. She had to work back to the Kelly case to understand the McKinley case. She was convinced that there was a connection. Robert Blackwood seemed to be the common

90

denominator. She got up.

"Well, thank you Luisa, you've been a great help."

Luisa got up and shook her hand. "It's okay. I hope you do catch your killer, if it's not your friend."

Donna opened the front door and turned to face her. "It's not Mark. These murders are not the work of some madman. There was a serious motive, and Mark has no motive."

She closed the door and walked out to the car.

The phone at the Kane house was ringing. It was noon, and Mark Kane was watching television. He hit the mute button on his TV remote and picked up the phone.

"Hello."

"Hi, Mark Kane? This is David Lemming. Remember me?"

"I'm trying hard to forget."

"Listen, I need to talk to you. Can you meet me?"

Kane sat up. "What's this all about?"

"Can't say over the phone. Meet me at Rudy's around say, seven thirty tonight."

Lemming hung up the phone.

Kane hung up, his mind racing. Why would Lemming want to meet him? Maybe he had found a new lead in the case? He certainly had to meet him. For some reason, he felt that if anyone could solve the case, David Lemming could. He turned around to see his wife lead a man into the living room. He had been expecting him. It was the lawyer, Donald Watts. He got up and shook his hand. Watts immediately got down to business.

"Mark, I'm only here because of my interest in this case. You see I prosecuted Michael Barnard in the Kelly case in 1990. He was acquitted. I never believed he was guilty anyway. The evidence was bullshit and so was the motive. I'll stick to my guns that the motive to that murder was either revenge or fear."

"Fear?" Kane asked skeptically.

"Yes, fear. Fear of being unmasked, given away. She knew something, and it got her killed."

"What's your feeling on my case?"

Watts smiled. "What's your feeling?"

"Well, I know I didn't do it. This witness is bogus. I certainly didn't kill the Kelly girl either."

Watts kept smiling. "Then how do you account for the fingerprints? Why would this witness lie? It's a known fact that

92

McKinley did drugs and possibly traded sex for drugs. Why shouldn't that drug supplier be you?"

"Because it just wasn't me!" Kane shouted. "I'm an engineer, not a damn drug dealer. I'm being set up."

"Are you? Who'd want to do you harm?"

"I don't know. Look, why exactly are you here?" Kane was growing impatient.

Becky came into the room and sat down. She had a worried look on her face. Watts looked at her and then looked back at Mark.

"All right," he said. "I'll tell you this. There is definitely a link between the two murders. One murder led to the other."

"Well thank you Sherlock Holmes," Kane said acidly. "Any other brilliant revelations?"

"Look here Kane, you're in trouble. I'm here because I want to help clear it up. Sarcasm isn't going to help your cause."

Kane ran his fingers through his hair. The stress was starting to get to him. He was much more irritable lately. His wife didn't tell him so, but he knew it. He let out a deep breath.

"Okay, I'm sorry. How can you help?"

"To begin with I tried to track down this mystery man in the brown Toyota that supposedly took some pot shots at McKinley on the day of the murder."

Kane leaned forward in anticipation. Watts continued.

"I asked around the neighborhood. A neighbor told me that he saw this car. He even gave me a description of the man driving it."

Kane nodded. "Yes, Pat Layman. Chief Davis told me about this witness. But he didn't tell me about any description."

"Who do you think informed our esteemed chief?" Watts asked. "Anyway, I didn't give him the description, because I wanted to check it out myself. You see Mark, I'm not a bad detective when I want to be. I have come across some unsavory people in my time. Ron Layman described someone who sounded very familiar to me, so I looked something up. Guess what I found?"

"What? Go on!" Kane was breathless. Becky was also a little excited.

"I found a hit man named Travis Singleton. He had just

been released from prison after serving five years. He matched the description I got. He lives downtown, so I decided to visit him. I sent him up the river, so he would know me. Anyway, he wasn't home, so I asked around. He drives a brown Toyota Corolla, and he even bought a gun from a local hood lately."

Becky Kane was livid. "How can anyone sell a gun to a former criminal?"

"Anyone can get a gun, Mrs. Kane."

Mark Kane was subdued. He did not say anything.

"Well Kane, what about it?" Watts asked. "Let's go visit the guy."

Kane shook his head. "What good would that do? All it would prove is that he may have taken some shots at her that morning. If we can't place him at the murder scene we can't say he stuck a knife in her throat."

Watts rolled his eyes. "You engineers are supposed to be logical? Don't you get it? He's a hitman! Whoever hired him is the man we're after, not him!"

"Or woman," Becky put in.

"Thanks Mrs. Kane, but now is not the time for equal rights speeches," Watts said dryly. He turned to Mark. "Let's go, we'll twist his arm a little, pressure him to talk."

Kane laughed. "Watts, who do you think I am? Fucking James Bond? For that matter, look at you. You're an old man. You'll get yourself killed trying to intimidate some hitman. I think we'd better call chief Davis and..."

"Davis wouldn't go for what I have in mind," Watts said sharply. " Besides, as I told you, I'm also a detective. I can handle myself in a tough situation. You are in deep shit, my friend. If I were you, I'd take any chance I had of clearing my name. I guess you think that justice will prevail and you can sit back and relax. I got a newsflash for you, Kane. Doesn't always work that way."

Kane was silent for a minute. He weighed his options. He had never been an impetuous and reckless type. Thus, this idea did not appeal to him at all. He was a family man, and liked to be safe at home with his wife and kids. However, Watts was right. He did not have many options. He was in deep shit, and sinking fast. Maybe it was time for him to take charge of his own fate. He got up.

"Well Watts, what are you sitting around for? We have a hitman to run down."

Watts smiled and got up. "I knew the man lurked in there somewhere. Let's go."

Becky got their jackets and the two men set out. The day was slightly overcast, and a light rain was falling. Watts was driving his tan Mercedes.

"He lives on Oakton. Apartment B-16. I asked his neighbors, and they said he stays in on Sundays."

As they got on I-70, he instructed Kane to get out a couple of guns from the glove compartment. Kane got them out and whistled. They were new Beretta nine-millimeter automatics.

"You don't fool around, do you?"

"I protect myself. Prosecuting attorneys aren't very popular with criminals."

"You know, I keep trying to figure out why someone would want to frame me for murder," Kane said. "I'm an engineer, my world is numbers, materials, and computers. I don't deal with drug dealers, pimps, hookers, gangs, whatever."

Watts nodded. "I really think it's a case of convenience. You were at the wrong place at the wrong time."

"What do you mean?"

"I've learned that during the time of the murder, you claim to have been eating at a restaurant."

"Yes, a co-worker of mine called me and asked to meet me. We were going to have a working luncheon."

"But your friend Donna did not think it was he who called? I wonder..."

Kane's face showed surprise. "You know quite a lot don't you?"

"I leave no stone unturned. That person who called you was the killer. He set you up to take the fall, and like a cow going to the slaughterhouse, you went."

"But why me?" Kane asked, annoyed at the reference to the cow.

"Maybe because he had something with your fingerprints on it. Thus how convenient it would be for him for you to not have an alibi during the murder."

Kane sat upright in his seat. "You mean that glass! But

95

how..."

"How could anyone get a glass with your fingerprints on it? It'd be easy to do at work, wouldn't it? You eat at the cafeteria, I am sure. Who do you eat with?"

Kane's eyes narrowed. "Just Donna. Sometimes Nate, sometimes Marty. Sometimes even James. Are you suggesting that..."

Watts looked over as he drove. "We come back to Nate again. Tell me, what do you know about this Nate?"

"Nate? Oh, he's a typical corporate boob. He's a paper pusher, although he thinks of himself as an engineering manager. He really hasn't done any practical engineering in years. Probably doesn't know how to use a damn screwdriver anymore. He'd probably ask you what a vernier caliper was."

"Oh, so you two are the best of friends?" Watts was sarcastic.

Kane laughed. "Well, I guess I think he's an asshole, but he's okay really. Harmless."

"Harmless," Watts echoed. "And yet he calls you and sets up a bogus luncheon meeting. Possibly swipes a glass with your fingerprints on it and sets you up for murder."

"Well, hold on now. He may not have been the one who called. It was probably someone on the outside. My lawyer is checking up on that," Kane said. "As for the glass, it could have come from someone else, or even somewhere else."

Watts got off the interstate and got on Oakton boulevard. They passed Broadway, and then pulled into the parking lot of an apartment building. It was a run down high-rise. A sign on the wall read:

SUNSET APARTMENTS - ROOMS FOR RENT

"He's not making much money, must not be a good hitman," Kane observed.

"Obviously so, he missed the girl didn't he?" Watts said, stuffing his gun in his jeans. He instructed Kane to do the same.

"You know how to fire one of these?" he asked.

"Good time to ask," Kane said. "Actually, I do. I learned to fire guns in college. Course called handgun safety 101."

"Did that course include this type of shit?" Watts asked as they stepped into the building. There weren't many people about. The place was a mess. Piles of newspapers lay strewn about the lobby floor. A seedy looking man stared at them from behind the front desk.

"Can I help you gentlemen?" he asked in a grungy voice.

"Does Travis Singleton live in this building?" Watts asked.

The man looked at a sheet of paper. "B-16. Take the stairs to the second floor. The elevator doesn't work." His voice was right from the bowels of hell.

"It doesn't work. No kidding," Kane muttered.

They ran up the stairs to the second floor. Apartment B-16 was right across from the stairs. Watts rapped on the door. There was no answer. He knocked a little louder. There was still no answer.

"Maybe he's not home," Kane suggested.

The door to the apartment beside them opened. An old black woman looked out.

"Who are you lookin' for?"

"Ma'am, we're looking for Travis Singleton, he lives here," Watts said politely.

"Ain't he answerin'? He ain't gone nowhere. Saw him come in last night drunk as can be. I'll bet he's passed out in there right now. Lord, that man's gonna go straight to hell one day, mark my words!"

"Thank you ma'am," Watts said and drew his gun. The woman screamed and slammed her door shut.

"Shit!" Kane shouted. "What did you do that for? She'll probably call the cops!"

Watts laughed. "You think the cops come here? Listen, I heard a noise in there. We're going to have to break the door down."

Kane shrank back. "No way! I'm in enough trouble with the law already!"

"What are you afraid of? They'll add more time to your multi-life sentence? Come on, I'll take responsibility."

Reluctantly, Kane agreed. They both started kicking the door. After a few minutes, it gave in and swung inward. Watts burst in, waving his gun. Kane followed him in, his grip on his gun

97

firm. He looked around. The place was extremely run down. The walls were full of posters of naked women. Watts went into the kitchen. He stopped in his tracks and looked down.

"What's up?" Kane asked, walking into the dirty kitchen himself. He stopped and stared. Watts was looking at the foot of the dining table in the middle of the kitchen. A man lay there. There was a bloodstain on the right side of his head. Watts grabbed his wrists to test for a pulse, and turned away in disgust.

"Is it Singleton?" Kane's heart was in his throat.

"Yeah," Watts was grim. "This is bad. This is very bad."

Kane sat down at the table. "What do we do now?"

"Don't touch anything," Watts warned. "I'll call the police." He went over to a wall phone and dialed a number.

Kane looked out the window. The front pane was open. It was a door style window that opened outward. He went over to it and looked out. They were on the second floor, but the drop down to the ground was not very high. He thought that he could jump out of it if he had to. Squinting his eyes, he noticed that a portion of the grass below was trampled with a pair of unclear footprints. They appeared to be fresh. There was also a pair of handprints in the mud beside it. Whoever had jumped had used his hands to stabilize himself, Kane thought. It was a good thing about the rain, because without it, these prints would not show up.

"What are you looking at?" Watts was suddenly standing beside him.

Kane pointed out his discovery to Watts. He nodded approval.

"Good. This proves it wasn't you. Singleton wasn't murdered too long ago, and you've been with me all morning."

"It only proves that I didn't kill Singleton," Kane said sadly. "You think this was done by the same guy?"

"Of course. Someone found out that Singleton knew something and shut him up."

Kane was puzzled. "What could he have known?"

"He knew who hired him to take a potshot at the McKinley girl. Ten to one that this guy is our mastermind."

Kane slapped the back of a chair in frustration. "But this means that we're back to square one."

"Not so fast! We'll still have Teresa Brown to question."

"We'd better get to her before she gets waxed too," Kane said.

Watts laughed. "Gets waxed? You've watched one too many cop-shows my friend. That would be a bad move for our killer. She's a prime witness against you."

"If she was killed, who would they suspect?" Kane asked.

Watts thought for a minute. "You."

Sirens wailed outside as three police cars pulled in. An ambulance arrived simultaneously, and in a minute Chief Chandler Davis walked into the apartment. At the sight of Watts and Kane, he shook his head in disbelief.

"Can't stay out of trouble, can you Kane?"

Watts pointed at the dead body. "Got a present for you," he said. "And it's not even Christmas."

As the police and paramedics milled about, Davis dragged the two aside.

"You two find the body? At the same time?"

"That's right," Watts said, "You arrested the wrong guy, Chandler. Looks like your real killer's claimed your third victim. Mark was with me all morning, and we found this guy very soon after he was killed."

"Who was this character?"

"Driver of the brown Toyota," Watts explained. "Seems like our psycho-nut got to him before we could. He was a hired hitman, but obviously not a good one."

A policeman came over and handed Chief Davis a notepad. "We found this by his phone, chief. What do you think?"

The chief read the top page. It read as follows:

"DAVIS (CHIEF)-555-1710 EXT 10 - WARN ABOUT GIRL."

Davis looked up in surprise. "Well, looks like I found out who my mysterious caller was!"

Kane frowned. "But chief, why would a person who had just taken shots at the girl call the police and warn them that her life is in danger?"

Davis ran his fingers through his hair. "Maybe he got nervous. We can see that he's not a good hitman."

"It's possible he missed the girl on purpose," Watts added.

Davis looked at his watch. "My minds getting completely

99

twisted in knots," he said. "It's way past lunchtime guys. Let's go grab something. We have a lot to discuss."

Watts and Kane agreed. Surveying the area once more, Davis joined them and the three men left the building. Lunch would be at Branson's.

Branson's was about a ten-minute drive from downtown, and as Watts parked his car by the side of the road, the men had forgotten about everything but their stomachs. Kane stepped out on the street side. He did not notice a blue pickup truck gather speed and head right for him.

"Look out!" Davis yelled.

The warning was too late, but the truck suddenly skidded away from Kane and sped off. Kane was still standing, motionless. Watts ran out in the street, cursing. Davis was already writing something down on his notepad.

"Idiot! I got his license number," he said. "Texas plates. SLX-199. He won't get far."

"Texas?" Kane was surprised.

Davis nodded, turning to Davis. "I need to use your car phone."

"Go ahead."

Davis climbed back into the car and picked up the cell phone. Soon he was talking to the police.

"Who's that? Askew? Listen, I need you to run a make on a 1993 Ford Ranger, metallic blue, license SLX-199. Texas plates."

"Hang on a sec, chief. It'll take five minutes," came Askew's reply.

Davis waited patiently. Outside, a small crowd that had gathered began to disperse. Presently, Askew's voice came back over the phone.

"The truck belongs to a Scott Kelly, sir. He's twenty-seven. Works as a bartender at Swizzer's. Moved here five years ago. Lived with his sister for two months, then moved out. Has been living at 1212 New Berlin road."

"What's his sister's name?" Davis asked sharply.

"Virginia Kelly, sir. Deceased."

"Have someone pick him up."

"On what charge, sir?"

100

"No charge yet. Just questioning."

"About what, sir?"

"Make something up!" Davis yelled and hung up. "You got to tell these damn young kids everything!"

He got out of the car. "You heard? Virginia Kelly's brother. Interesting, isn't it?"

Kane nodded. "Think he was trying to kill me?"

"We'll see."

"Why didn't we just chase him down?" Watts asked. "We could have caught him, pressured him to talk, and..."

"I'll give you three reasons why we didn't," Davis said, cutting in. "First, he had too much of a head start. Second, I saw no reason to endanger innocent lives by leading us through a dangerous high-speed chase through a very busy section of Denver. We'll get him anyway."

"What's the third reason?" Kane asked

"The third reason is the most important one," Davis said, leaning in and lowering his voice to a whisper. "I'm hungry."

Lunch at Branson's was uneventful, and when Kane was dropped off at his home in the afternoon, he was as confused as ever. He had hoped that Davis would clear some things up for him, but all he did was make it clear that he was still a suspect and pending trial. He did give hints that he really didn't believe in Kane's guilt. This gave Kane some relief.

He walked into the living room and sat down on the couch. The remote control was at his fingertips, so he flicked on the television. Looking at the wall clock, he saw that it was 3:35. He remembered David Lemming's phone call. He had certainly been eager to meet him tonight. He wondered why. Had Lemming seen the error of his ways? Had he found some new clue that would prove him innocent? Kane smiled. No, he probably had not. He probably wanted to meet him for an entirely different reason. He wanted to pick his brain. Kane was scowling now. No way that arrogant bastard was going to get the best of him. He'd play it cool.

Suddenly, Kane's thoughts were interrupted by a ringing sound. He came back down to earth with a start. It was the phone.

"Hello."

"Mark. It's Donna."

101

Kane brightened. "Hey! How's it going?"

"I'm in San Antonio. Can't talk too long."

"What's up?"

"I'm going to talk to Brad Kelly and his ex-wife, Margaret Kelly-Smith."

"Oh, they're divorced?"

"Yes, for three years. Happened three months after Virginia's death."

Kane frowned. "That's strange. You'd think a daughter's death would bring a couple together more."

"So you'd think. Anyway, Knoxville was a success."

"What did you find out?"

"I found out that Blackwood could have a very strong motive."

"What's that?"

"Listen Mark, I have to go now, I'll tell you all about it when I get back."

"There's been another murder, Donna."

After a second, Donna spoke. "Who?"

"A hit man named Travis Singleton. The guy in the brown Toyota."

"Who did it?"

Kane laughed. "That's the million dollar question."

"Ok, gotta go. Bye!"

He hung up. His wife came into the house with Trish and James. She had a handful of groceries. He got up to help. Trish threw his arms around his legs. He knelt down and gave her a kiss. He had always spoiled her, but she was his little girl.

"Hey dad, mom says that things are going to be okay," she said, grinning.

Kane stroked her hair. "Of course, sweetheart. Things will be fine."

She ran up the stairs, with James following her up. Becky came out of the kitchen and looked at him carefully.

"How are you? How was your day?" she asked.

Kane looked her in the eyes. "There was another murder."

Becky's eyes froze. "Who?"

"A hitman named Singleton. He was the guy who tried to shoot the McKinley girl."

"I don't like this Mark," Becky said in a concerned voice, "Are we safe? Are the children safe? There's a madman running around, and you're neck deep in it."

"We're perfectly safe," Kane said reassuringly, "As long as I am a suspect, he wouldn't do anything to jeopardize that."

"Small consolation."

Kane pulled his wife in close to him and looked into her eyes. She looked back at him and smiled.

"Thanks," he said softly.

"For what?"

"For being there."

She smiled. "Hey, for better and for worse, right? What did you expect?"

He kissed her. "Nothing less."

She fell into his arms. The next few moments were theirs.

At seven thirty that night, Kane pulled his car into Rudy's. It was a suburban sports bar, and not his kind of place. He was not a blue-collar person, and Rudy's was a blue-collar bar. He wondered why Lemming had chosen this place to meet him. Walking in, he immediately was struck by the brightness of the place. He squinted and read the neon beer signs and sports logos on the walls. There were at least thirty television sets in the place, and they were all tuned into a baseball game. Kane looked around. The place was fairly crowded. He spotted David Lemming in a corner booth. As their eyes met, he smiled and waved. Kane walked over and sat down opposite him.

"Evening Mark. Nice night."

"Yeah."

"Want a beer?"

"Sure."

"Miss!" Lemming yelled out to a waitress, " A Michelob light for my friend."

The girl came back promptly with the beer and Lemming paid her. Kane took a swig and faced him. Lemming lit a cigarette.

"I thought you didn't like smoking," Kane said.

Lemming blew smoke into the air. "Just don't like unfiltered ones like that bozo chief Davis. You into the Rockies?"

Kane shook his head as if to say no.

"I think they'll do well this year. Hayes and Galaraga are dynamite. I am not sure about their pitching though. The bullpen will..."

Kane cut in quickly. "Did you drag me here to discuss baseball? Let's cut through the bullshit, Lemming. What do you want?"

Lemming smiled broadly. "What do I want? What makes you think I want anything?"

Kane sighed. "I'm not in the mood to play games."

"All right," Lemming's smile vanished. "It's very simple, Kane. I've been snooping around some."

"I'm not surprised. Go on."

Lemming blew smoke into the air. "You're a member of Eastgate Health Club?"

Kane stared. Where was he going with this?

"I mean, you don't go much, but you're a member."

"Right. So what?"

"Your locker number is twelve?"

"Correct. Would you like to know my underwear size?"

Lemming did not laugh. "I found this in your locker, " he said, producing a piece of folded notebook paper. "I got an anonymous tip that it would be there."

Kane looked at the piece of paper. It was a letter:

October 17th, 1990

Darling,

I'm sorry to have to write this letter in such an impersonal way, but I couldn't face you and tell you this to your face. I have to break off this thing we have. It can't go on. I have found out about you and I can't go on with a man that would cheat on anyone. Please understand it's for the best. I have been trying to shake off this cocaine habit for the past month and I think I can do it. Continuing a relationship with you won't help me do that. I hope you understand. Love,
Virginia.

Kane looked up. Lemming's eyes were dancing. He threw the letter in his face.

"This proves nothing, Lemming."

"It was in your locker, Kane."

"I've never seen it before!"

"There's something else," Lemming said, digging in his pocket. "I took the liberty of searching in your office desk."

"You did what!" Kane exploded.

Lemming ignored the outburst and produced a torn piece of paper. On it were the words, "Kill the bitch."

"Is that your handwriting?"

Kane laughed. "Oh for Pete's sake, that was just a joke. I was just jotting down a list of things on my agenda. Haven't you ever said I'm going to kill someone before?"

"A joke?" Lemming echoed. "I fail to see any humor in the words 'kill the bitch', Kane. Must be your warped sense of humor. Or maybe you're right. It was a list of things on your agenda."

"No, you don't understand..."

"I understand this," Lemming said coldly, "Three people have been murdered. I have a letter connecting you with Virginia Kelly days before her murder. The evidence against you is clear in the McKinley case. The only thing that remains now is your confession."

"I'll never confess," Kane said stoically.

Lemming's smile came back, and he took a sip of his beer. "I think you'd better. Things will go easier on you if you do."

"Damn it, I'm innocent," Kane said desperately. "That letter could be to anyone, my name's not on it. Try tracking down your anonymous caller. He's your murderer."

Lemming laid back in his seat. He lit another cigarette and thought about something. His face was like stone.

"I know you're the murderer Kane," he said slowly. "Just a matter of time before I prove it."

Kane shook his head. "You can't prove it, Lemming. You want to know why?"

Lemming leaned forward. "Why?"

"Everything you have is circumstantial. That letter has no name on it. The fingerprints alone won't get me."

"What about the witness?" Lemming asked. "You never did tell me how you knew it was a she."

Kane smiled. "I'm psychic."

Lemming did not smile. "She's a pretty solid witness, Kane."

"Solid? Chief Davis thinks that she's lying. That's enough to create a doubt right there, " Kane said. "So you see, all you really have is squat."

"So you admit that you did it?"

"I admit nothing, Lemming," Kane said. "I'm just putting the challenge to you. If you think I did it, go for it. Prove it. Otherwise, shut the fuck up and let me get out of this shithole sports bar."

He got up to leave. Lemming grabbed his hand.

"Bravo! Good show!"

"What?"

"Looks like you got some balls after all."

Kane looked blank.

"Sit down, Kane. Don't go away mad."

Kane sat down again. Lemming's expression had changed dramatically.

"I wanted to test you. Get your reactions."

"You what?" Kane was bewildered.

"I was suspicious about the phone call too. Too convenient. Then when I found the letter, it was obvious. Someone's trying to frame you."

"Are you playing games with me?" Kane asked, astonished at the turn of events.

"I don't play games," Lemming said sharply. "Now listen. Whoever is trying to frame you is good. I did get that call, and I did find this letter. That was no lie. Did you ever call your friend Nate?"

Kane frowned. "How did you know about..."

Lemming stopped him with a wave of his hand. "I know everything. So you haven't called him."

"No, my lawyer was going to do that. I haven't heard from him today."

"Good," Lemming said. "That should be our first move. We have to determine who the hell called you for lunch that day. He's the same person who killed the girls and is paying off this Teresa Brown woman to lie in court."

"Paying off..." Kane was speechless.

106

Lemming laughed. "Of course! Do you think that a woman who works at Gates third shift assembly line and makes five twenty an hour can afford to live at Deerfield lane? I checked it out. Her rent is six hundred and fifty a month. That nice mustang she drives? She claims it was a present from her brother. I checked that out. She has no brother. Plus, she gets no alimony. The breakup was completely her fault."

Kane was still stunned. "But that means that..."

"It means that someone has been planning this murder for a long time. He got cold feet and hired a hitman. He botched the job, so he did it himself, all along establishing you as the murderer. He even pays off Miss Brown to say that a guy with your description and car was in the apartment at the time of the murder. He then plants a glass with your fingerprints on it at the scene, a few pieces of lint, and a bogus love note in your locker. This guy's done his homework, Kane."

Kane was staring down at his beer, completely transfixed in his seat.

"What a setup."

Lemming nodded. "You see Kane, I don't leave loose ends. That love note is still a mystery. Who was it to? Joe Thurman, her fiancé'? A lover on the side? Asking around at your health club didn't help. No one there is very observant."

"We can't all be snoops like you, Lemming."

Lemming grinned. "Have another beer. We've got an important thing to do tomorrow."

"What's that?"

"We're going to visit Teresa Brown and apply a little pressure. I think that we can crack her."

"You mean you haven't done so yet?" Kane asked with some malice in his voice.

"No. I've been slacking too much," Lemming said solemnly, "But we'll do that first thing tomorrow morning."

Kane took a sip of his beer. "Let me ask you a question. Why didn't you tell me all this sooner? How much of this does chief Davis know?"

Lemming grinned and lit another cigarette. "That's two questions."

The waitress came around with another round of drinks.

Kane looked at her and frowned. Something was bothering him. Some type of memory.

Lemming flicked some ashes in an ashtray and spoke. "The truth is, I didn't tell you all this sooner because..."

Kane was not listening. "What is this drink?"

"It's a beam and a coke. Straight whiskey drink from Kentucky," he said appreciatively. "You like beam?"

"This is what I had at the airport," Kane said, staring at his drink as if it was the strangest thing he had ever seen.

Lemming scowled. "What are you talking about?"

"I had a drink at the airport bar the day I picked up my wife at Denver International."

"So?"

"So don't you see!" Kane got excited, "I had a drink! It was before the murder! The glass had my fingerprints on it!"

Lemming looked skeptical. "Are you suggesting that the bartender is our elusive killer?"

"No, no!" Kane said impatiently, "I had a conversation with a rather strange man at this bar. Suppose the meeting was no accident? Suppose he followed me as his scapegoat? Suppose he stole my glass? He could have, I left the glass on the bar right there in front of him."

"Well, I..."

"What were the contents of the glass? I know it was analyzed!" Kane was practically on edge.

"Well, it did have a trace of whiskey and water, but..."

"That's it!" Kane exclaimed, "This guy's name was ... John Kirby. That was his name. Why don't we look him up and..."

Lemming interrupted him. "John Kirby? Are you sure that was the name?"

"Yeah. He wore a wig. I think he had a fake moustache too."

"Describe him," Lemming was suddenly very serious.

Kane scratched his head. "Well, he was very average. Hard to describe. Very strange personality though. Fancied himself a womanizer."

Lemming's eyebrows shot up. "Womanizer?"

"Yes, he seemed to think of himself as a ladies' man. Said he liked to live off rich women and then leave them."

"Oh, a real sweetheart huh?" Lemming said, smiling.

Kane nodded. "He even said that if a woman were to ever stalk him, he'd get rid of her."

"Macho bullshit?"

"I don't think so," Kane said. "This guy was creepy."

Lemming was thinking. "You know, four years ago I met a John Kirby. He came around on the night of the Kelly murder. I thought he was a little suspicious at the time, but we never heard from him again."

"Are you kidding?" Kane was incredulous, "That places him at the first crime!"

"There's something weird though," Lemming said slowly. "The guy I met had no moustache, and was a fairly good looking fellow."

"Well, I'd say a wig and a moustache would change the looks of a person dramatically," Kane insisted.

Kane finished his drink. "We need to find that bartender. Ask him what that guy did with your glass that night. He must have seen."

"Let's do that after visiting Teresa Brown tomorrow," Kane said.

"We'll have to be cautious," Lemming said, "You're still a suspect in the eyes of the law. Wouldn't look good for you to be visiting the key witness against you."

Kane got up and got ready to leave. He put some money on the table and laid his hand on Lemming's shoulder.

"Call me tomorrow morning."

Lemming smiled. "I will. Good night."

Kane marched out of the bar, feeling a lot better that he did when he had walked in.

San Antonio

Donna Houseman got up and shook hands with Brad Kelly. She was at the country home of the fifty five year old lawyer in the outskirts of San Antonio, Texas. Now as she sat down in the spacious living room of the rancher, her host poured her a drink. She studied him carefully. Quite a good-looking man, she thought. His hair was dark, with streaks of gray. He was about six foot two and looked like he worked out extensively. A real cowboy lawyer, she thought, smiling to herself. Brad Kelly handed her a glass of sherry and sat down.

"Miss Houseman. So nice to meet you. You're even prettier than you sounded on the phone." Kelly's voice was warm.

Donna smiled. "Thank you sir. I'd like to ask you a few questions about your daughter."

"You get right to the point don't you? Very well, I'll try and be helpful."

Donna took a sip of her drink and got out her notepad. "How would you describe your daughter?"

"She was a very sweet girl. Very smart and goal oriented. She was quite popular, and had a lot of friends. She was the all American girl." There was a surprising lack of emotion in Kelly's voice.

"She was engaged to be married was she not?"

"There's a joke," Kelly said. "She was engaged all right, to Joe Thurman. It was all appearances though. Joe slept around, and she did too. She really wasn't ready for marriage."

"So why get engaged?"

"Like I said, for appearances. Virginia wanted the image of a nice conservative girl, but that was a mask. She was sweet all right, but wasn't ready to settle down."

Donna looked up. "Tell me something about Joe Thurman."

Brad Kelly sighed. "He's your typical male, sweetheart. All he's looking for, and will forever look for is a young pair of legs to

110

conquer." He leaned closer to Donna. "I even have the feeling he may be bisexual."

"Is that right?" Donna tried to not show her surprise.

"Possibly. I'm just speculating."

Donna was puzzled by Kelly's attitude. He did not seem bothered by any of what he was saying. She said so. Kelly laughed.

"Why should I be bothered, girl? You can only raise your daughter till she's eighteen. After that, whatever she does is up to her. Whatever she did got her killed."

"And what did she do?"

"Oh come on Miss Houseman, you seem like a bright woman, you figure it out." Kelly was smiling broadly.

"You're not much of the grieving father, are you?"

Kelly stopped smiling. "Look Miss Houseman, I loved my girl. However, it happened four years ago. I don't dwell on the past. Life goes on."

Donna nodded and said, "Tell me about your son."

"Scott's always been a loser," Kelly said in an indifferent tone. "He flunked out of college and went to some bartending school. He moved up to Denver and stayed with Virginia a few years ago. I think he's working some dive in East Denver now. I'm sure he does drugs. He lives in a motel room, so his official address is still mine, right here in San Antonio."

"What was his relationship like with Virginia?"

"I spoke with Chief Davis in Denver over the phone about that," Kelly said. "You see, Scott was adopted by me and my ex-wife, Margaret. He was sixteen or so when we adopted him. He had been in and out of homes all his life. We thought we could be a stable force in his life. You can't change a Chevette into a Rolls, though. He didn't change much. He did have some incidents with Virginia. She caught him trying to peek at her when she was changing clothes. He was always trying to touch her. We sent him to a shrink, and it worked to some extent. Then Virginia went away to college."

"And then Scott moved up there with her for a few months?" Donna asked.

"Yes, but she kicked him out for some reason she wouldn't tell us. I imagine it was for the same reason. Scott even threatened Joe."

111

"So his feelings for his step-sister went beyond brotherly love?"

"I guess so," Kelly admitted. "It's really not that unnatural though. It's not like they grew up together. They didn't see each other much, so the brother-sister feeling was probably not there."

"That's very interesting."

"No, you think it's disgusting," Kelly said, looking into Donna's eyes. "I can't say that I blame you. Scott couldn't help himself though. He had a rough childhood."

"Mr. Kelly, is Scott prone to violence?"

"You mean could he have been jealous of Joe Thurman enough to kill Virginia? The answer is no. Yes, he could be jealous, and possibly could ponder killing someone. But he's too stupid to plan something like that. Plus, he really wouldn't have the guts to do it," Kelly said, taking a deep breath. "You see Miss Houseman, in the bigger picture, Scott could only kill someone on the spur of the moment, if he was angry enough."

Donna was writing frantically. She wished she knew shorthand. She looked up at Kelly. "Have you ever seen him lose his cool?"

"Yes," Kelly said, nodding. "Once when he was in high school, he got angry at a friend of his for drinking out of his milk carton. He bit the shit out of him."

"Bit him?"

"Yes. Scott does have some problems, Miss Houseman. He is not, however, a cold-blooded killer. You're barking up the wrong tree."

Donna put her pencil down. She had heard what she needed. She did not like Brad Kelly at all, and wanted to leave. The whole unconcerned attitude he had about his daughter's death bothered her. She got up to leave.

"Leaving so soon?" Kelly asked, somewhat surprised.

"Yes. I have to call on your wife Margaret in twenty minutes."

Kelly smiled. "Ex-wife," he corrected.

"Sorry."

"It's okay. But listen Miss Houseman, if you're going to be here tonight, how about dinner? I know a great Tex-Mex place on Commerce Avenue."

"No thanks Mr. Kelly," Donna said, opening the front door. "I'm sure I'll be tired tonight and go to bed early. I have a plane to catch tomorrow morning."

"Oh well, your loss," Kelly said arrogantly. "I've got to say, you're the prettiest P.I. I've ever met."

"I'm not a P.I., Mr. Kelly. Good day," Donna said and shut the door behind her. She looked at her watch. She had fifteen minutes to get to Margaret Smith's house. It was thirty miles away. She got in her rented Grand-Am, hoping traffic wouldn't be bad.

Margaret Kelly Smith was a small birdlike woman who looked to be in her late forties. She wore a great deal of makeup, and had that distinctive Texas drawl when she talked. As Donna introduced herself, she immediately started taking a liking to this woman.

"Come in dear, have a seat," Smith crooned. The house of Troy and Margaret Kelly Smith was just west of San Antonio. The area was distinctly suburban and had a strong Mexican flavor to it. As Donna looked around the spacious Spanish style home, she thought she could definitely live there. The place had warmth and character.

"I'm sorry Troy's not in, he's in El Paso on a meeting. These businessmen are always on the move!"

Donna smiled. "What does he do?"

"Oh, Troy's a salesman for Rayburn Plastics. He's always flying around," Smith answered in a half-hearted manner.

Donna looked up at the living room wall at a picture. "He's a handsome man."

Margaret Smith was pleased. "Isn't he? I never thought I'd fall for a younger man, but he proved me wrong."

"How old is he?"

"Troy's thirty two. I'm forty something."

Donna grinned. "You don't look it," she said politely, although she thought that she definitely looked it.

"It doesn't matter really. We're very much in love," Smith said, changing her tone. "Now, what are you here for, dear?"

"Well, I'm here to ask you a few questions about the death of your daughter four years ago."

The woman's face clouded. "What do you want to know about that? That is still a very painful subject to me."

"I know that, Mrs. Smith, " Donna said softly. "However, I represent Mark Kane, the man who has been accused of the murder of another woman. Chances are, the murders are related."

"You represent the man who killed Virginia?" Smith asked sharply.

"No ma'am. Mr. Kane is innocent. He is the victim of an elaborate frame up job. I'm trying to determine who the real killer is."

Smith's face did not change. "What do you want to know?"

"First, what type of marriage did you have with Brad Kelly?"

Margaret sighed. "A good one, but one lacking any passion. He brought home the bacon, but we were never really close. After Virginia's death, we drifted apart more, and within a year we got divorced."

Donna pinched her upper lip. "I talked with Mr. Kelly earlier today. He didn't seem overcome with grief."

Margaret nodded. "That's Brad. He lacks emotion and passion, Miss Houseman. At Virginia's funeral, he didn't shed a tear. His philosophy in life is there's no time for wasted emotion. It's so unnatural and inhuman."

"What's your opinion of what happened?"

"You mean Virginia's murder? Oh I'm pretty sure Joe did it. Joe was two timing her and wanted out of their relationship."

Donna shifted her weight. "There are ways out of a relationship other than murder, Mrs. Smith."

"You don't know Joe. He is the devil, he is. He'd sell his own grandma if he thought it'd bring him anything."

"So you're certain it was Joe Thurman who killed your daughter?"

"My bet would be on him," Margaret's eyes started to water. She grabbed a tissue from the side table and blew her nose. "And he got away clean."

"Mrs. Smith, I'm sure you've heard of Frank and Lynne McKinley?"

"Oh sure!" Margaret's face lit up, "I know Lynne quite well. Their daughter was a friend of..." she stopped suddenly, her expression changing. "Why do you ask?"

Donna took a deep breath, "Because their daughter was

recently murdered in Denver."

Margaret said nothing. Her eyes fell to the floor.

"You were not aware of this, Mrs. Smith?"

"My God," Margaret whispered, "Are you saying her murder might be connected to Virginia's? Is that why you are here?"

"It's a possibility. The murderer's M.O. was the same. Of course it raises the possibility of a serial killer, but with so many similarities and connections, I doubt it."

Margaret Kelly Smith suddenly sat up straight. She looked Donna straight in the eye.

"Did you know that Joe sells drugs? Did you know that Virginia almost overdosed on heroin in 1989, thanks to him? Did you know that Traci McKinley also did drugs? Can you put two and two together?"

"Mrs. Smith, there has been no connection made between Joe Thurman and Traci McKinley, except for the fact that he knew her due to being Virginia's boyfriend," Donna stated.

"You have no idea!" Margaret Smith said, her voice rising a little. "Joe Thurman is your man. If I were you, I'd have him arrested, put him in the chair, and pull the lever."

Donna was taken by surprise at the viciousness coming from this small and frail woman. She stood up and stared out the window. "Look, Mrs. Smith, we can't pass judgment on someone with no proof. We're no judge of..."

"He'll kill more people if you don't put him away."

Donna decided to switch gears. "Tell me about your son, Mrs. Smith."

"Scott? He's a frail and weak boy. He was a frightened teen-ager when we adopted him. Instilling self confidence in him was our biggest problem."

"Was he a violent person?"

Margaret laughed. "Violent? Scott? No, Scott has a gentle nature. He hated violence, even on television. Why, whenever he'd see blood on the..."

Donna interrupted. "Mrs. Smith, was Scott in any way infatuated with Virginia?"

Margaret Smith bit her lips. "I was hoping you wouldn't ask that question. I guess you could say he was. It really wasn't

115

unnatural though. He wasn't really Virginia's brother. They only saw each other after school, and then Virginia went away to college."

"I understand Scott moved up there with her for a few months."

Margaret nodded. "Yes, she put him up until he could find a job and a place to live."

"But why Denver, Mrs. Smith? Why didn't he go somewhere else?"

"He had a sister there. He was tired of San Antonio, and wanted a change."

Donna leaned forward. "Is Scott a jealous type of person?"

"Oh yes," Margaret said, "He is very definitely that. He has a very complicated mind you know. He's not crazy though. Just a little misunderstood."

"Was he jealous of Joe Thurman?"

"Oh I'm sure he was. He hated anyone Virginia dated," Margaret said and then came to a realization. "But he'd never hurt anyone for that."

"I see, " Donna said, somewhat skeptically, "How do you come to know the McKinleys?"

"Oh, Lynne and I met each other through Troy's dad. His dad used to be a professor at UT-Knoxville, and retired recently. We met at a party they threw for him. Apparently Troy's dad is a good friend of Frank McKinley."

"That's interesting that you know each other, and both your daughters went to the same school and were murdered," Donna said slowly.

Margaret Smith sighed loudly. "One of those strange and tragic coincidences of life, I guess."

"I wonder," Donna mused.

"Mark, wake up, it's chief Davis on the phone."

Mark Kane awoke with a start. His wife was standing over the bed, smiling at him. He looked at the bedside clock. It was 7:20.

"Damn, what does he want? I gotta go to work!"

Reaching over, he grabbed the cordless.

"Hello, Kane here."

"Kane," Davis's voice boomed, "Get your ass over here if you want to see us question the guy who tried to run you over."

"Scott Kelly? You got him?"

"Of course, " Davis said nonchalantly, "He's nervous as shit too. It'll be fun."

"How can I..."

"You'll witness it. We'll ask him questions behind a one-way mirror. You'll see and hear us, but he won't see or hear you!"

"I should go to work."

"Kane, you better get your priorities straight. I think your boss might forgive you, considering you're in the middle of a murder investigation."

Kane sighed. "I'll be there in thirty minutes."

"Be here in fifteen."

By the time Kane got downtown, it was almost eight. He rushed into Davis's office. He wasn't there. A bearded police officer came in and asked him what was going on.

"Where's Chief Davis? I was supposed to meet him here."

"He's downstairs in the interrogation room. You may go down, he's expecting you."

The man started to leave. Kane called after him.

"Hey, how do you know who I am?"

The officer smiled. "Are you kidding?"

Kane shook his head and marched down the flight of stairs. He barged into interrogation room number two. As he came in, he

117

saw Davis sitting at a chair. A woman police officer sat beside him. Kane saw a room at the other side of the window. A skinny and nervous looking man was being questioned by Detective Walker. Davis saw Kane and motioned for him to sit down. Kane pulled up a chair.

"Where have you been?"

"Traffic," Kane replied, "What's happening?"

"That's Kelly. Walker's got him rattled already. Shut up and listen."

"...So you do own a blue Ford Ranger with the license number FPX-3397," Walker was asking.

Scott Kelly was extremely nervous. "Yes, but listen. I..."

"Mr. Kelly, are you aware that trying to run over an individual with a vehicle is attempted homicide?"

Kelly turned pale. "L-l-look, I wasn't really trying to kill him."

"Then what are you trying to do?"

"I wanted to kill him, but I couldn't, so I swerved and missed."

Walker got up and started pacing. He shook his head vigorously.

"I'm sorry Mr. Kelly, but that is just no good. No sale. I can get you right now for attempted murder. You'll get ten to twenty, even possibly..."

Kelly broke in. "Look, I was upset, he killed my sister you know!" His voice was starting to get high pitched.

Behind the window, Davis cracked a smile. "Boy's a damn wreck."

Walker spoke up. "He allegedly killed her, Mr. Kelly. He is innocent until proven guilty."

"Look, what would you do if your sister was killed by some damn nut?"

"I wouldn't take the law into my own hands, Mr. Kelly," Walker's voice was stern. "What you did is not excusable."

Kane looked at Davis. "I want to talk to him."

Davis made a face. "What for? Just press charges, and we'll throw him in jail. The guy's admitted he did it, he's a loser. Let him rot."

"I want to talk to him," Kane repeated.

Davis shrugged. "Whatever," he said, and spoke into a microphone. "Walker, let Kane in, he wants to talk to him."

"Alone. No one else watching," Kane said firmly.

Davis stared in surprise. "What! We can't let you talk to him alone. He tried to kill you!"

"What are you suggesting, he'll try again?"

"No, I'm suggesting you might try to kill him."

Kane smiled. "Trust me, chief."

"Kane, you're still a suspect you know. But I'll back off, you can talk to him in room 14."

Walker took Scott Kelly to room 14. Kane quickly slid in after he was left alone. As he entered the room, he saw Kelly pacing. He stopped in his tracks and stared at Kane. His mouth flew open.

"Surprised to see me?" Kane asked in a low voice.

Kelly said nothing. Kane pulled up a chair and sat down at a table that was full of computer equipment. He invited Kelly to do the same, and he also sat down, trying not to look into his eyes.

"Well, I'll come out and say it," Kane began, "You tried to kill me yesterday. In the eyes of the law, that's a crime. I could send you to jail for a long time. I will, however, make you a deal. I'll not press charges if you tell me who paid you to do so."

Kelly looked amazed. "Paid me? Nobody!"

"You acted on your own?"

"Yes, but I really didn't try to kill you. I missed on purpose. I just wanted to scare you."

Kane scowled. "That's not exactly what you said a few minutes ago."

Kelly bit his lip as he realized that Kane had witnessed his questioning. He looked down at his feet and started scratching the back of his head.

"Why did you want to scare me?" Kane asked, his voice low and intense.

"I thought you had killed my sister four years ago."

"But you don't think so now?"

Kelly looked up at Kane. "You don't understand," he said, his voice filled with emotion. "I loved my sister. She was murdered by a ruthless and brutal killer. They never caught the son of a bitch. So when I read in the paper that a similar murder occurred, and it was a girl that my sister knew, I went nuts. I wanted to kill you immediately."

"So why didn't you?" Kane's face was expressionless.

"Because I'm not a violent person, Mr. Kane. It took all I had to try and scare you. I would never have run you over."

Kane looked at the pathetic little man in front of him. He was inclined to agree with him. He didn't look like a killer.

"Do you believe me, Mr. Kane? I did not try to kill you."

Kane waited a moment before replying. "Yes, I believe you Scott. But now you must answer some questions for me."

Kelly sighed. "All right."

"You were adopted at age sixteen by Brad and Margaret Kelly. At that time Virginia was almost seventeen. What was your relationship with her?"

Kelly looked down at the floor. "As far as she was concerned, I was a troubled younger brother."

"And what about you?"

"I had a crush on her. Ok, to be honest, I lusted after her, like any sixteen year old boy who had just met her would."

Kane was calm. "And how did this make you feel?"

"What are you, a shrink? I hate shrinks!"

"I'm not a shrink, Scott," Kane said evenly, "Just answer the questions, you owe me that much."

"Well, how do you think I felt? A little ashamed, very confused. Then, in a year, she went away to college."

"You yourself came to Colorado to live after high school. Why?"

"To be with my sister," Scott Kelly answered. "I even lived with her for a few months, trying to get my feet on the ground. She didn't like it, but she couldn't throw me out in the streets."

"Why didn't she like it?"

"She knew how I felt about her. I think that was one reason she moved to Colorado. It's not like there aren't good schools in Texas. She wanted to get away from me," Kelly said, smiling. "Then here I come, moving right on back into her life."

Kane pressed on. "What happened then?"

"After a few months, I got a job at a local bar, so I moved out."

Kane raised his eyebrows. "You moved out?"

Kelly sighed. "Okay, I was kicked out. I guess Virginia got a little sensitive about the incident..."

"What incident?" Kane asked sharply.

"It was nothing, really. I walked in on her and her damn boyfriend."

"Joe Thurman?"

Kelly shook his head. "Hell no. It was some other guy. She slept around. It was probably some drug pimp she hung around with."

Kane frowned. "What type of drugs did she do?"

"Anything she could get her hands on. Heroin, weed, speedball, cocaine, acid. You name it, she's probably done it."

"This drug dealer you walked in on, could it have been Dan Martinez?"

"No, Martinez was a Hispanic guy. This guy was white."

"You have no idea who it was?"

Kelly thought for a moment. "I didn't get a good look at the guy, but you know, I have a feeling that I've seen him since then."

Kane thought this was leading somewhere, so he continued. "Do you know a man named John Kirby?"

"Doesn't ring a bell."

"What about Robert Blackwood?"

"No."

"Joe Thurman. What are your feelings towards him?"

"He's a damn druggie too. The guy's an asshole."

"He was your sister's fiancé."

Kelly laughed. "What a joke. That marriage would have lasted about a month."

Kane leaned forward. "Now I'm going to ask you a question. I want you to answer me objectively. Take all prejudice away from your mind. In your opinion, who killed your sister?"

Kelly was silent for a moment. "I don't know. I don't think it was you though. Not any more."

"I'm glad to hear that."

"I'll tell you who has the temperament to do it. Joe Thurman."

Kane studied Kelly closely. "Is that who you'd like it to be?"

Kelly smiled broadly. "You're very astute, Mr. Kane. I

121

would indeed like it to be him. I can't stand the man."

Kane nodded. "I'm glad you're leveling with me. It's too bad we don't have our proverbial smoking gun."

Kelly grinned wryly. "That would be too easy."

Kane stood up. "I'm not going to press charges against you, Scott. In the future, try not to jump to conclusions before you have the facts. And even if you do have the facts, don't try to run people over with your truck. You're not very good at it."

Kelly stood up and shook his hands. "Thank you Mr. Kane. You're a good man. Believe me, I'll never try a stunt like this again!"

As he left the room, Kane looked at his watch. It was ten o' clock. He went upstairs to Davis's office. Davis was sitting at his desk, biting on a pencil. Kane sat down noisily in a chair.

"Biting pencils now, Chief? Hypertension isn't good for your health."

Davis took the pencil out of his mouth. "The hell with your hypertension. What happened?"

"I had a nice talk, which I'm sure you recorded. Play it back."

Davis's face fell. "You're not pressing charges, are you?"

"The guy made a mistake. Let's cut him some slack."

Davis fell from the sky. "I can't believe this shit, Mark. The guy tried to kill you! You're just going to let him walk?"

"He didn't try to kill me. Just got a little emotional. I try to do one good deed a day."

"But the guy tried to kill..."

"No, he tried to scare me. And in so doing, he's allowed me a chance to talk to him and gain some valuable information."

Davis crossed his arms. "What information?"

"Something about the past."

"Could you be more vague, please?"

Kane laughed. "Look chief, I have got to go. I have to meet someone this morning, and I'm probably late." He left the chief, still frowning.

There was a pay phone in the hall. Kane put a quarter in it and dialed a number. It was picked up after two rings.

"Law office of Phil Wellington, this is Diane."

"Diane, it's Mark Kane. Let me speak to Phil please."

"Phil's in a meeting with a client right now, Mr. Kane. Could I have him call you back?"

"No, just leave him a message for me," Kane said, thinking Phil didn't pick secretaries because of their voice inflection. "Tell him I asked about the phone call to Nate. Have him call me at home this afternoon."

The secretary said she would relay the message. Kane hung up and dialed another number. This time an answering machine greeted him in David Lemming's voice.

"This is the Lemming residence, please leave a message. Kane, if this is you, where have you been all morning? Meet me at Deerfield apartments number two. Our Miss Teresa Brown lives there."

Kane smiled and hung up. Lemming knew that he'd call. He grew more impressed with the man. He was prepared for anything, it seemed. He walked outside, got into his car, and got on the interstate.

By the time Kane was parking his Volvo in front of the apartment that Teresa Brown occupied, it was ten forty. He looked around. A new mustang was parked in the spot designated for apartment two. Teresa Brown was in. He decided to wait in the car for Lemming to show up, since his beat up car was nowhere to be seen. He looked at the door of apartment number one. There was still yellow police tape on it. He shuddered. This was it. This was the place where the murder had taken place. A chain reaction of events had taken place, and now he was sitting in his car merely feet from where the murder had taken place. He looked at his watch again, getting restless. It was nice and sunny outside, so he decided to get out of the car. Why not try and get a peek at her, he thought. He walked up to the door of apartment number two.

David Lemming swung his car up to apartment number two. He saw Kane's Volvo there, with Teresa Brown's Mustang beside it. He stepped out. Kane was nowhere to be seen. He walked up to the door. It was partially open, so he stuck his head in. Still seeing no one, he drew his gun and walked in carefully. The apartment was furnished with ugly furniture and expensive paintings on the wall. He looked at them and grimaced. Such a waste of money. He was never a big fan of the impressionists. He groaned at the trash all over the floor. Typical slob. He walked into the kitchen noiselessly. There was an empty plate on the dining table with a half full glass of some liquid in it standing beside it. He sniffed at it. It smelled sweet and pungent. Grapefruit Juice, he guessed. He drew back the shades of the adjacent window. Turning, he saw the flight of steps going upstairs. He decided to see if anyone was there. He walked up the stairs quietly and saw one bedroom door ajar. He peered in.

Mark Kane was bending over a woman's body. The body was lifeless, that he could see immediately. There was a knife going through the throat. As he tried to get a better look, his foot hit the door with a thud.

Hearing the sound, Kane leaped up and turned around. Seeing Lemming, a look of relief came into his face.

"David, look what's..."

Lemming aimed his gun at Kane and spoke sharply, "Kane, what's going on here?"

The look of relief was replaced by surprise. Kane drew back, suddenly aware of the situation. He fumbled for words.

"Listen, I... I just found this woman here a minute ago. Our... our killer I guess beat us to her."

Lemming did not lower his gun. "How long have you been here?"

"About five minutes. Listen David, I..."

"Why are you inside the apartment? Who let you in?"

"No one," Kane said, regaining his composure. "The door was open. I just knocked, and when no one answered, I came in to investigate."

Lemming reached down and touched the body, his gun still aimed at Kane. "The body's still warm. She's not been dead too long."

Kane scowled. "Listen, if you think I killed this woman..."

"What am I supposed to think, Kane?" Lemming's tone was acid, "I walk in to see you bent over a dead body with a knife in her throat. You've already knee deep in another murder investigation. Now the woman who is the big witness against you is dead."

Kane was somewhat shocked. "But what about our

conversation yesterday? You said that you were sure that I was being framed."

Lemming picked up the phone and dialed the police. "Yes, but this looks bad, Mark. Real bad. Hello? Let me speak with chief Davis. This is David Lemming."

A few minutes passed, and Lemming was talking with the chief. Kane looked around. There was a heavy trophy of some kind on the dead woman's dresser. He looked at it carefully. It could do the job. He made up his mind.

Lemming was still talking on the phone. "Yes chief, Deerfield lot number two. You've met her before I believe."

Behind him, Kane's voice rang out. "David, I'm sorry..."

He swung around, but was too late. A heavy, metallic object came crashing down on his head. He saw black. The phone receiver fell from his hands.

Davis was still on the line. "Hello? Hello!"

Kane picked up the receiver and hung it up. He was nervous. He glanced once at the dead body of Teresa Brown and checked the pulse of David Lemming. He was alive, but there was a big cut across his forehead. He ran down the stairs and out the front door. The Volvo started up and he backed up in a hurry, slamming his rear bumper into a parked car. There was no time to waste. He shifted to drive and sped away.

About half an hour later Lemming awoke. He was in an ambulance. He looked about in alarm and tried to get up, but a paramedic held him down.

"Sir calm down, you've been in an accident."

"Accident my ass!" Lemming flared up, "I have to talk to chief Chandler Davis right now, let me go!"

"Not now sir, you need to be examined first. You can talk to him later," the paramedic said with a tone of finality.

"Damn!"

Lemming lay back down, his mind racing. What exactly had happened? He remembered; the dead body, Kane leaning over the body, getting whacked over the head. He closed his eyes.

Later on, after the doctors were through looking at him, he was given seven stitches across his forehead. He begged to be released, but the doctors wanted him to stay overnight for fear of a

125

possible concussion. He reluctantly gave in, and was whisked away to his room.

Chief Chandler Davis strode into the room of David Lemming. It was one thirty in the afternoon. Lemming looked up from his bed and smiled.

"Well hot shot, what happened to you?" Davis was smiling.

"Got conked by Kane as I was talking to you on the phone."

Davis was surprised. "It was Kane? Are you sure?"

"Positive. I'm surprised, though. I was beginning to think that he hadn't done it. Now it looks like he's pulled a fast one on us."

Davis sat down on a stool. His face was serious. "What exactly happened today?"

Lemming took a deep breath. "I had arranged with Kane last night to meet at Teresa Brown's this morning. I called him around nine, but he wasn't home. His wife said he'd rushed to the police station."

"That's right, he was with me," Davis said.

"Anyway, I hung around some more, called him again, and got the same story. So, I decided to get some breakfast and go on down to Teresa Brown's house myself. I left a message on my machine for Kane just in case he called. I went down to Java's, got some breakfast, and then went down to the apartment."

Davis broke in. "What time did you arrive there?"

"Around ten fifty. I saw that the door was ajar, so I walked in. I walked up to the bedroom and saw Mark Kane bending over the dead body of Teresa Brown. I questioned him, and he got fidgety. I decided to call you, and when I was on the phone, I heard him say something. I turned around, and the next thing I knew I was waking up in an ambulance."

Davis was thoughtful. "Do you think he killed the woman?"

"I'm not sure what to think."

"Let's see. Kane left the P.D. at around ten fifteen or so. It's about a fifteen or twenty minute drive from there to the Brown apartment. That means that he probably got there about fifteen or ten minutes before you did..."

"He said that he'd only been there five minutes," Lemming

126

said.

"Well, that's a matter of five or ten minutes discrepancy. Could be explained by a number of factors. Now let's see..."

"Where is Kane now?" Lemming asked.

The chief looked up. "I don't know. He's disappeared. I called him at home. He was not there."

"He's been playing me for a fool," Lemming said disgustedly. "I was really starting to believe that Joe Thurman was behind all this shit..."

"Thurman's being brought in again," Davis said. "Get this though. Blackwood's flown the coop."

Lemming sat up. "Blackwood? The fashion model himself?"

"Yeah, I tried to contact him last night. He's nowhere to be found. I called all the girls he says he dates. No one's heard from him."

Lemming pinched his lip. "I might as well let you know. There's a connection between Kane and Virginia Kelly."

Davis waited. Lemming went on. "There was a love note that I found in Kane's locker at his gym. It was a note from the Kelly girl. She was breaking it off with him."

Davis was aghast. "Why didn't you tell me all this before?"

"Because I thought he was being framed by a clever murderer. It never occurred to me that he might be trying to make himself look too guilty."

"You mean plant evidence against himself to make it look like he was being framed?"

Lemming nodded. "Yes, the old reverse psychology trick. He can't be guilty! He would be too stupid to leave all these clues lying around! I'll bet he made that call to me himself."

"What did this caller sound like?" Davis asked.

Lemming thought for a moment. "Deep voice. Sort of a southern accent, but somehow not quite."

"Like it was someone trying to mimic a southern accent but doing a bad job?"

"Exactly!"

Davis's eyes lit up. "Kane went to school in Atlanta."

"You suppose..."

Davis stood up and started pacing. "One thing bothers me,"

he said, furiously stroking his chin, " Why? Why? Why the hell would a prominent engineer at a growing company kill a twenty eight year old nurse? Why would he kill a student four years before? Why would he kill a bumbling hitman? Why would he kill a wretched woman making minimum wage at a rubber company? I tell you, it doesn't make sense! We're missing something!"

Lemming lit a cigarette. He blew out a cloud of smoke and said, "Dig deep chief. Dig into the past. That's where the answer lies."

Davis swung around. "What are you saying? He killed Kelly because of something he shared with her in the past?"

"He grew up in Atlanta. He went to Georgia Tech. Traci McKinley grew up in Knoxville. She knew Kelly. Their folks knew each other. These two cities aren't very far from each other. You add it up, and there has to be a connection in the past!"

"We need to question that friend of his, Donna Houseman. She'd know things about his past," Davis said slowly.

Lemming nodded, taking another hit off his cigarette. Davis stared out the window.

"Okay, so why did he kill McKinley?" Lemming asked in a hushed voice.

"McKinley hinted to me that she may have witnessed something. Perhaps she walked in on Kane and Kelly in a not so compromising position?"

"So Kane waits four years, and then all of a sudden kills her?" Lemming was skeptical.

"Maybe she was blackmailing him, and he finally got tired of it."

"That's possible," Lemming said, looking at Davis carefully, "Kane then kills Singleton who he'd paid at first to do the dirty job, but who had bungled the job, and was shaky. He then paid Brown to say she saw him. He knew she was flaky and could be dismissed as a weak witness, making his case better. But how do you account for Thurman and Blackwood? And what about John Kirby? Who is this mystery man?"

"John Kirby?" Davis was puzzled.

"He was supposedly the stranger that Kane met at the airport bar. He told me that he'd had a drink at the bar with this guy. This was the same person that was at the Kelly murder scene

128

twenty minutes after she was found."

Davis looked even more perplexed. "I have never heard of such a person."

"I know," Lemming said with a chuckle. "It's probably nothing. He is a mystery man, though. I suggest you question the bartender at the Mile High bar."

"I will," Davis said, getting ready to leave. " I have to go talk to Thurman. As far as Blackwood is concerned, we'll see if he turns up."

"Don't forget this Houseman chick," Lemming yelled as Davis ducked out the door.

As the door slammed, Lemming lit another cigarette and smiled. He leaned back in his bed. Things were getting very interesting.

When Chief Davis got back to his office, Donna Houseman was waiting for him there, along with Kane's lawyer, Phil Wellington. Davis showed surprise at seeing them.

"Well, looks like you two are a bit late, aren't you?"

"Late for what?" It was Donna who spoke.

"Your boy's disappeared. He killed Teresa Brown, conked Lemming on the head, sending him to the hospital, and vanished from the face of the Earth."

Wellington looked like he had fallen from the sky. "What!"

Davis sat down and explained the situation to them. Donna Houseman shook her head. "No, chief. It's still not right."

"Murder is never right, Miss Houseman," Davis said sharply.

"I meant..."

"I'm glad you're here Miss Houseman," Davis broke in, "You've known Mr. Kane for a long time?"

"Twenty four years," Donna said.

"Anything you can share about him when he was in college? Did he do something that no one but you knows about?"

"No. Mark's always been a straight arrow. He hardly even partied in college. He barely ever drank, and never touched drugs."

Davis sat down on his table and faced the two opposite him.

"Did he know the Kelly family? Brad or Margaret Kelly?"

"No. However, Frank and Lynne McKinley know them. Does that strike you as odd?"

Davis thought for a moment. Then he said, "A little. How do you know this?"

"I've been doing a little investigating of my own. I've spoken to the McKinleys, Kellys, and a woman named Luisa Gutierrez."

"Who's she?"

"Traci McKinley's high school best friend. She even went to college with her, where they went separate ways. She's got a child. Guess who's her father?"

Davis waited patiently.

"... Robert Blackwood," Donna finished.

Davis threw up his hands. "What does that prove? We know Blackwood got around. Big deal!"

"Blackwood knew all three women," Donna said calmly, "He had intimate relations with all three women. To me, he has to be a suspect, as I am sure we can dig up a motive in that bizarre triangle...sorry rectangle. As for these new murders that happened while I was gone, he was covering himself."

Davis licked his lips. He was feeling confused now. This case had way too many connections here and there. There were too many intimate relationships and webs for his taste. He liked his cases to be clear-cut.

"Well, I'd like to question Blackwood too, but he's vanished as well," he said, somewhat tentatively.

"Can I say something?" It was Wellington who spoke. "I had a talk with this Nate Goodman person. It seems that he did not call Mark on the day of the murder. He had meant to, but forgot. And, he said that he would have never agreed to eat at Branson's. Too pricey."

"I see," Davis smirked, "Goodman's a Jew."

"I'm a Jew," Wellington said quietly.

"No kidding? With a name like that? I'd have sworn you were..."

"What would you like my name to be? Aaron Goldstein? Or perhaps you'd like to change your name to Hitler?" Wellington said tartly.

Davis backed off. "Listen, I was joking, I..."

"Can we discuss religious stereotypes in American culture later?" Donna said impatiently, "We did come here to see you about something, Chief."

Davis looked embarrassed. He sat down and motioned her to continue. She did.

"We came here to tell you that Scott Kelly could also have a hand in this, as well as Blackwood and Thurman."

Davis shook his head and smiled. "More suspects huh? Maybe it was none of the above? Maybe it was the butler? Or maybe it was Batman?"

Donna did not smile. "Look, we are serious here! A man's life..."

Davis held up his hand. "I know all about Scott Kelly. He attempted to run over Kane yesterday with his pickup truck. Chickened out at the last second."

"What! You mean he's here in jail now?" Donna asked.

"No. Kane refused to press charges."

Donna was shocked. She turned to Wellington. "Did you know about this?"

Wellington shrugged. "Not a clue."

A police officer poked his head through the half open door. "Sir, a Joe Thurman to see you."

"Show him in here. These people will stay."

The officer disappeared. A minute later Joe Thurman walked into the office with an air of nonchalance. He smiled and closed the door behind him.

"Nice to see you again, chief."

"Have a seat, Mr. Thurman."

"Oh, please call me Joe," Thurman said, turning to Donna and Wellington. "Uh, who are they?"

"These people are involved in our little murder case. Their names are not important," Davis said, trying to sound somber.

Thurman smiled again, but this time it was a mocking smile. "Chief, why is it that every time you question me there are strangers around?"

Davis leaned back in his chair. "I thought you'd like the attention."

"Okay, let's cut the bullshit," Thurman said curtly, "What do you want?"

"Mr. Thurman, do you know a Scott Kelly?" Davis asked.

"Of course. He's Virginia's brother."

"Do you know of his feelings towards your late fiancé'?"

Thurman frowned. "Feelings?"

Davis shifted in his seat. "You aren't aware that Scott Kelly was adopted at age sixteen? He was attracted to his step-sister ... your late fiancé'."

Thurman started laughing. He laughed real hard for a minute.

"What is so funny, Mr. Thurman?"

"Nothing," Thurman said, still amused. He tried to regain his composure. "I'm just trying to picture that little weasel trying to scam on his step-sister."

"And that is funny to you?"

"Yes, because it is so ridiculous. Scott hated Virginia. Virginia didn't much care for Scott either. She only put him up for a few months because he was her step-brother."

"Mr. Thurman, Scott Kelly himself admitted that he had a thing for his stepsister. He said that it was something that he felt immediately after he met her."

"He's full of shit, or sick. Take your pick."

"Mr. Thurman, you were asked last time if Virginia cheated on you. I have a feeling that you know that she did. Do you know who it was?"

Thurman looked uncomfortable. "If she did, and I'm not saying so, I have no idea with whom."

"Do you know a Robert Blackwood?"

"Never heard of him."

"Is it possible he was Virginia's lover?" Davis asked, leaning forward.

"I just told you I've never heard of the guy. She could have been having an affair with King Kong, as far as I know. I didn't keep tabs on her. Why are you asking questions about our love lives anyway? Didn't get your fill of soap operas this week?" Thurman's face showed irritation.

"It's pertinent to the case," Davis said.

"It's bullshit," Thurman said, "Virginia was killed by some God damn sicko serial killer who'd probably seen one too many slasher flicks. The same happened to that other babe a week ago.

132

End of story."

"How well did you know Traci McKinley?"

"She was a suitemate of Virginia's. We talked a few times."

"Did you know she did drugs, like Virginia?"

"Not my concern."

Donna spoke up from across the room. "Mr. Thurman, let me ask you a question. How do you feel about Mr. Margaret Kelly?"

"Virginia's mom? She's weird. Don't care much for her. Why?"

"She doesn't care much for you," Donna said. "She thinks you killed her. I think she may have a point."

Thurman was not fazed. He chuckled. "What makes you think that I care what she, or you, think?"

"It's not important that you care," Donna said coldly. "What you need to know is that if you did this, you are going down."

Thurman was cocky. "You're scaring me, Miss Sherlock Holmes. I suppose that I should be shaking in my shoes now that you're on my trail, whoever you are. Is Perry Mason there helping you?" He pointed at Wellington.

"Look, threats are going to get us nothing," Davis said, thoroughly annoyed, "What we need is the truth, and we need it now!"

Thurman was silent. Donna looked at her watch and said, "This is a waste of time, chief. We need to find Blackwood."

"And Kane," Davis added.

Thurman got up to leave. "Are you through asking me meaningless questions? If you no longer feel the need to hassle me, I'll be going."

"Don't leave town," Davis warned as Thurman slammed the door behind him. Donna shook her head.

"That guy's very obnoxious," she said.

"We have to keep our eyes on him," Davis said and picked up the phone on the table in front of him. "Send in the bartender."

Noticing the questioning looks on both his guest's faces, Davis explained to them about Kane's story about the bartender and the man at the airport bar. As he was finishing, a rather fat man walked in. He was a black man with a face that was too round for his proportions. He had a large handlebar moustache on his face.

Davis judged him to be in his late thirties.

"Have a seat, sir," he said.

The man was nervous. He sat down as told and looked at the three people in front of him. He did not say anything. Davis tapped on the table with his finger.

"What's your name?" he asked, looking the large man straight in the eyes.

"Tyrone Love."

"Occupation?"

"I'm a bartender at Mile High bar, sir."

"That's at the airport?"

"Yes sir."

"Did you work the evening of last Sunday?"

Love thought for a moment. "Yes I did, sir."

"Please stop calling me sir."

"Okay sir."

Davis smiled. "Mr. Love, do you happen to remember a couple of men who had a drink at your bar that day, say around five thirty or six that afternoon?"

Love was startled. "Well sir, I get a lot of customers, it's hard to remember..."

Davis pulled out a picture and handed it to the man. "This is a picture of one of the men. Recognize him?"

Donna looked over his shoulder. It was a picture of Mark Kane. Love slowly nodded.

"Oh yeah, I do remember him and that guy."

"You do? Why is that?" Davis said, suddenly excited.

Love put the picture down. "Because this man had a very strange conversation with another guy that he met at the bar."

"What was the conversation about?" Davis pressed on.

Love thought back carefully. "Well, I only caught parts of it, but there was no one else at the bar, so I couldn't help but listen."

Davis said nothing.

"Anyway, the had a conversation that started off plain. Then this other guy started saying that he was a womanizer, and that women were silly putty in his hands, and so on. He said something about he'd never let one get the upper hand on him."

Davis and Donna exchanged glances. Blackwood?

134

"What did this other man look like?"

"White guy. Average Joe, but I think he was wearing a wig and a moustache. Didn't act like he belonged there."

"What does that mean?" Davis asked sharply.

"Well, usually I can tell whether a man's at the airport to receive someone or taking off somewhere. Call it bartender's intuition," Love explained, "This guy looked like he was there for some other purpose."

"So what happened after their conversation?"

"The guy in the picture got up and left. The weird guy had another drink and left as well."

"He just left? You didn't notice anything weird? Nothing missing?"

Love looked up at the ceiling, thinking. "You know, now that you mention it, I did think that he stole the other guy's glass, but I brushed that off as too weird."

Davis sat up straight. "You were missing a glass?"

"I thought I was."

Davis reached into a drawer and brought out something wrapped in plastic.

"Would it be this glass?" he asked, watching Love's reaction carefully.

Love's eyes widened. He pounced on the package, looking at it carefully.

"This is our glass! Where did you get it?"

Davis smiled in satisfaction. "That's not important. What is important is you trying to give me a better description of this man."

Love was confused. "Why did he steal a glass? He didn't look like he was poor or anything."

"Can you describe this man any better? Think!" Davis was not to be denied.

Love thought for a minute. He licked his lips. His expression was not revealing.

"Like I said, he was very plain looking. About six feet tall, hundred eighty or so pounds, wore a white shirt..."

"Did he strike you as the womanizer type?" Davis asked.

Donna spoke up. "Could it have been a good looking guy dressed up to look plain?"

Love smiled, flashing a remarkable set of white teeth. "Did

135

you have someone in mind?"

"She may have," Davis said, "However, we can't really pinpoint anything much from your description. Did he have any distinguishing features, like maybe a tattoo or a scar?"

Love shook his head. "Sorry, but I didn't see anything like that, but..." he broke off, as if suddenly hit by a thought, "Wait a minute! There was one thing I did notice about him! He had an extra finger on his left hand!"

Davis stood up suddenly and looked straight at Love. "You're saying he had six fingers on his left hand?"

"That's right. I noticed it clearly."

"This may be a break, but damn it!" Davis exclaimed, slamming the table with his fist. He turned to Donna and Phil Wellington. "We have to find Blackwood. He may be our mystery man."

"Anyone notice Thurman's fingers? I did not, " Wellington announced.

"That's because you're not a detective," Davis said, somewhat spitefully. "He had all five of his fingers, no more, no less."

Love was staring at Davis. Now he spoke with a bit of hesitation. "Uh sir, have I helped any?"

"Yes Mr. Love, you have been a great help," Davis said, shaking the man's hand. "You may have helped clear an innocent man."

"Can I go now?"

Davis nodded. "Thanks again. We will probably call on you again."

Love got up and said his goodbyes. He left the three in a very excited state.

"You know, Lemming's going to want more proof than that guy's word. Even his testimony wouldn't tell the courts much," Wellington said.

Donna was excited. "But this does prove that the glass did not come from Mark. That guy swiped the glass for only one purpose, and that was to plant at the murder scene. Therefore we can conclude he is the killer, and it was premeditated. Mark was in the wrong place at the wrong time."

"Question is, who is this guy?" Wellington said.

Davis picked up the phone and dialed an extension. "Fisher. Get me a make on John Kirby. Height about six feet, weight one eighty. Cross reference with one Robert Blackwood and let me know what you come up with."

Donna stared at him as he hung up. "Who is John Kirby?"

"He's our mystery man, Miss Houseman. That is, if Lemming is correct. I'd say it's an alias, and if so, he's probably our man. I'd bet my bottom dollar that Robert Blackwood and Kirby are the same person. Kirby was at the Kelly murder twenty minutes after the police got there. I think it was Blackwood, maybe checking out his handiwork."

Donna sat down, perplexed. This was news to her. The problem was now two-fold. How would they find Blackwood, and where was Mark Kane? She thought she knew where Mark was, but she didn't say anything.

Wellington said, "So chief, let us know when you find Blackwood."

Davis smiled. "No small task, but I have a hunch. Now Miss Houseman, I will leave it up to you to find Kane. I think he will contact you."

"Really? How do you figure that? I'd figure he'd contact Rebecca, if anyone."

"You know he will. I expect you'll do the right thing."

Donna said nothing. The chief was right, he would probably contact her before his wife, not wanting to drag his family into anything. Plus, she and Kane had a past, and the chief seemed to know it. Yes, if Kane were to call anyone, it would be her. She had already made up her mind what to do if that happened. Things were moving. There were not many options left.

"Can I help any?" Wellington asked.

"Yeah. There's a chance Kane might contact you too, Phil," Davis said. "When or if he does, tell him to turn himself in. He's doing no one any good hiding from the law."

"He's innocent you know," Donna said cheerfully.

Davis looked at her, his face breaking into a crooked smile. "We'll see!"

That evening Donna returned home in a muddled mood. She was not sure if things were looking up or not. She wished Kane had not run away. She parked her car in the driveway and took her time in getting to her door. She was feeling somewhat lethargic. She let herself in and went directly to the kitchen. Opening the refrigerator door, she looked inside. Good, she thought, there's still some orange juice left. She poured herself a big glass of the orange liquid and tasted it immediately. Good, it still tasted fresh. She loved the orange juice with the pulp in it. She made her way to her couch in the living room. She made herself comfortable and flicked on her television. As CNN flashed on the screen, she tried to put herself in her best friend's shoes.

Mark must have had a reason for running. He was never prone to violence, so he must have been desperate. A disturbing suspicion awoke in her mind. What if Mark was guilty? Could a person know another person totally? What if he really was running from the law for apparent reasons? Maybe the incident at the airport bar was a big set up by Mark himself. Maybe he set up a meeting with some hitman, or even possibly...

With a start, she awoke from her trance and scolded herself for doubting her best friend. Shame on you Donna, she told herself. Mark Kane is your friend, and you should not doubt his character. Right now he needs your support. She rose and went back to the kitchen for another glass of orange juice. As she shut the refrigerator door, the phone rang.

Mark?

She rushed to the phone and answered.

"Hello!"

"Hi Donna. It's Becky."

A sigh of disappointment escaped Donna's lips. "Oh, hi."

"I was wondering if you've heard from Mark yet."

Donna smiled. Becky knew her husband better than she thought. "No. I'd have called you if I had."

"So I guess he's officially missing now?" Becky's voice quavered a little.

"Well, not officially."

"He's vanished. Do you have any idea where..."

"Becky, I've been thinking about it. I do think I know where he could be. But I'd be doing him a disservice if I told you."

Becky was incredulous. "What? Donna, you tell me right now!"

138

"Listen Becky, you don't really want to harm him, do you?"

Becky was stung. "Well of course not, but I think I have the right..."

"Trust me, he's better off hidden right now."

Becky was silent for a moment. Then she said, in a low voice, "You know, it's sad. You're closer to my husband than I am."

"That's not true," Donna objected meekly, knowing full well that it was.

"It is true. You know him better. He knows you better. I'm surprised you two never married each other."

"Our relationship was never like that, Becky. We were always..."

"It's okay," Becky was calm,"I understand. What's important is that we both care for him, and I wish you'd tell me where he is."

"I'm not sure myself, Becky. I just have a feeling."

"Where?"

"A special place we went to when we were in college. A place we sneaked off to get away from our studies and our stresses. We always swore we'd go back there if we were ever stressed out beyond belief."

Becky was surprised. "But you two went to college in Georgia!"

"I know."

Donna took the exit off I-75 northbound into highway forty-one. She was in the town of Acworth, Georgia. She had landed at Hartsfield airport in Atlanta two hours ago. It had been difficult to get a couple of days off from work, but this had to be done. Now as she guided her rental car towards Allatoona Lake, she turned to her traveling companion.

"Allatoona Lake was our sanctuary," she said wistfully, "We went there to chill out. I remember clear starry nights at Hale's barn, right beside the lake. We'd bring the telescope and look at the stars and planets."

"Did you spend nights there?" Becky Kane asked, somewhat sharply.

"Oh yes," Donna said happily, "After many six packs, we didn't have much of a choice!"

"What else did you two do here?"

Donna sensed some hostility from Becky Kane. She turned to her and smiled reassuringly. "Don't worry. Our relationship was strictly platonic. I never slept with him."

"That's really hard to believe."

"It's true," Donna said, turning into a gravel road. They could see the lake on their left now. The water glistened in the early afternoon sun.

"It's beautiful," Becky said. "You're sure he's here?"

"Ninety percent," Donna said and made a sharp right turn. "There it is!"

The car stopped and Donna got out. Becky did the same, and stared at an old, dilapidated barn standing about twenty yards from the water's edge.

"That's your romantic barn?" she asked skeptically. The place did not impress her much.

"Yes. It was more mystical than romantic. Especially at night," Donna said in a nostalgic voice.

140

Becky looked around. "Doesn't look like he's here. I see no one."

"Let's go in," Donna said, opening the weather-beaten door. As it opened, the two women peered inside. There was not much inside. An old rusty lathe stood in the corner. A pile of rusty metal shingles lay beside it. The floor was overgrown with kudzu and other weeds. There were a few piles of rotten hay lying under a ladder that led up to a loft.

"As I said, he's not here," Becky said with a trace of disappointment in her voice.

Donna bent over and picked up something from behind the pile of hay. Becky walked up. It was a piece of paper. She looked at it closely.

"It's a hamburger wrapper. Generic too," she said.

Donna sniffed at it. "Fresh too," she said, smiling. "Onions and horseradish."

Becky stared. "Mark likes horseradish on his hamburgers!"

Donna turned. "I know. Let's go to the lakeside beach."

"He's here isn't he?" Becky was suddenly breathless.

"Of course."

The two women stepped outside and Donna led them down a small trail. It was obviously a trail created by people walking on the grass repeatedly. They stepped out into a clearing. There was suddenly sand underneath their feet. The lake was a few yards from them now. Becky stopped cold.

"He's not here."

Donna said nothing. She kicked a stray can of beer and winced as she realized that it was half full. The beer had spilled all over her shoes. She picked up the can and looked at it carefully.

Becky laughed. "What? Are you thirsty?"

"It's still cold," Donna said. "Someone's been here recently."

Becky brushed back her hair from her face and stared across the lake. It was a fairly large lake, but the other side was visible. Gently rolling hills painted the horizon.

"This area sure is pretty. I can see how it could be a place to get away from life."

Donna nodded. "Especially since not many people know about this beach. Everyone goes to a boat dock or the marina. Then

141

there's that enclosed area on the east side where you can swim."

Becky suddenly stiffened. She had a peculiar sense about knowing when she was being watched. That feeling was now invading her full force.

Donna sensed the change in her companion. "What's the matter?"

Becky lowered her voice. "I think we're being watched."

Donna smiled. "Of course we are. It's Mark."

Becky did a double take. "Where is he?"

"I don't know. I doubt if he wants to be seen. I'd say there's a good reason for it."

"Donna, if Mark is here, he'd want to talk to me."

"And do what? Make you an accessory?"

"Donna..."

"Listen Becky," Donna said seriously, "Mark is in trouble here. We believe he's innocent, but the law is not sure. I think he's better served staying here until this mess is cleared up. Let's just go back to Denver. He'll contact us when he's ready."

Becky's eyes widened in surprise. "But we came a thousand miles to see him!"

"No, we came a thousand miles to see if he was here. Now that we know he is, let's just..."

"We know what?" Becky interrupted, "All we've seen is a hamburger wrapper and a can of beer."

"That's all we need!" Donna's eyes were pleading. "Let's go. Now!"

Something in her tone made Becky look at her in surprise. Donna was on to something and whatever it was she was frightened. There was an urgency to her voice. She decided to press no further, and nodded in agreement.

Donna said loudly, "Well, looks like Mark's not here!"

Becky studied her face carefully. It seemed to be saying, "Agree with me."

"Yeah, you're right. Let's go back to Denver," she said in an equally loud voice.

They walked back up the trail that they had come and reached the barn. Donna jumped into the car and got it started. Becky stopped, took a glance around, and got in. The car spun its wheels on the gravel and sped off towards the main highway.

They did not say anything to each other until they reached the interstate and were heading south towards Atlanta. Finally, Becky spoke up.

"Okay, what happened out there?"

Donna stared straight ahead. "You were right. We were being watched."

"Did you see who it was?"

"No, but it wasn't Mark."

"What did you see?" Becky asked quizzically.

"I saw a man looking at us through binoculars. I saw the reflection of his lenses."

"Where? I didn't see..."

"He was in a car. Parked behind a bush."

"He was watching us?"

Donna made a face. "Did you see anyone else there?"

Becky was still confused. "But why would anyone watch us?"

Donna changed lanes to pass a truck. Passing it she said, "Maybe someone thinks we know more than we do."

"You mean..."

"I mean nothing. All I know is that someone was watching us. That means that they knew we were going there. We were probably followed, maybe even from Denver."

"Do you think Mark was there?"

"I think so. He probably saw us, I'm sure of it," Donna said, pulling into a rest area. "Listen, can you drive? My nerves are a little shaken."

Becky obliged, and pulled right back out. Now as she drove, she continued the conversation.

"If Mark saw us, why did he not get out and..."

"He probably saw that we were being watched and didn't want to expose himself."

Becky shook her head sadly. "I can't believe all this. I can't believe he was there and we didn't see him. We didn't even see a car!"

Donna said, "Mark knows the area very well. He can stay hidden there if he wants to."

Becky glanced at a roadside sign. Atlanta was only twenty miles away. She bit her lip. She had to do it. A quick turn of the wheel and she was in the grassy median. She turned the wheel violently and the car was on the northbound interstate again. A few cars honked wildly and sped around her through the shoulder.

Donna had been thrown about. Now she blinked. "What the hell are you doing?"

"I can't do it," Becky said breathlessly. "I can't just leave him there without talking to him."

"But what..."

"Donna, I have to see him. This is stupid, his being here. He needs to be with his family."

"Becky, don't be crazy. Don't you..."

"I'm not being crazy!" Becky shouted loud enough to surprise herself.

Donna raised her hands up in defeat and sighed. "So what is the plan?"

"I'm going back and finding him."

Donna looked out the back window and squinted. There was a pickup behind them. Becky looked at her.

"Worried about our friend?"

Donna nodded. "Remember, I don't think we were only being watched by Mark."

"That's a pickup truck behind us," Becky said, "You said our boy was in a car."

Donna stared at the rearview mirror. The truck behind them was taking an exit. She breathed a sigh of relief. Becky looked at her and laughed.

"Look at us! Who do we think we are, Thelma and Louise?"

Donna smiled. "I'm not going over a cliff with you!"

Their exit was coming up. It was almost six o'clock now, but being late April, the sun was still out. Becky remembered the way to the lake easily, and guided the car down to the barn with no problem. The two women got out and looked around. Everything still looked the same. Donna shook her head.

"We shouldn't have come back."

"I'm going in the barn," Becky announced and walked off. Donna followed her hesitantly. Becky opened the barn door with a loud noise and strode in.

"Mark! Are you in here?" She was startled by the echo of

her own voice.

Donna walked in and looked about. She was still nervous.

"I wish we'd get out of here, Becky."

"What are you getting so spooked for?" Becky said, annoyed now, "We're just looking for Mark. It's daylight outside. What could happen to us?"

Donna's face was grim. "I don't know. This place used to have a mysterious and romantic feel to it. Now all I get is an ominous dread."

Becky laughed. "You're flipping out, Donna. Stop watching late night television, okay?"

There was suddenly a thud as the barn door slammed shut. The two women watched, startled. A click sounded. The lock?

"Hey!" Donna shouted and ran towards the now closed door. She pulled at it, but it was shut tight. Becky came over to help, but it was no use. Someone had locked them inside the barn.

Chief Davis looked down at his watch. It was already nine o' clock. Another late night. He got up to leave. It was not to be, as Fisher walked in.

"Cross reference on the Blackwood and Kirby request done, sir," he said triumphantly.

"And?"

"Although the two seem to have similar outlooks on life, there is definitely a distinct difference between the two," Fisher replied, somewhat stiffly.

The chief sat back down. "This is going to be a long night."

"Shall I go on, sir?"

"By all means!"

"There is no John Kirby fitting our description, sir. There are six in Denver, two hundred in Colorado, and over two thousand in the country."

"And not one fit the description?"

"Not one that has six fingers, sir."

"Blackwood?"

"Blackwood was spotted at the Virginia Kelly murder, sir. In fact he was there soon after the body was found."

Davis let this sink in. "So he was at Kelly's murder, and he's McKinley's boyfriend. Have the guy picked up. I want him, I

145

don't care if he's in Pluto."

"He is missing sir, but there is an APB out on him as we speak."

"I know he's missing," Davis said, irritated. "What about Kane?"

"There's been no new development on his case, sir. However, his wife is nowhere to be found."

"What!" Davis almost fell out of his chair. "Why wasn't she being watched?"

"Bruno was watching her, sir. Yesterday evening, she called someone. She then got in her car and drove off. Bruno lost her on the interstate."

"Oh that's good. She probably would have led us right to Kane!" Davis stormed.

"There's a chance that she went somewhere with Donna Houseman, sir."

Davis frowned. "Don't tell me. She missing and we also lost her on the interstate."

"I don't know sir. We weren't watching her. Phil Wellington called this afternoon demanding to know if we knew where she was."

"Obviously not, since we're a bunch of incompetent morons," Davis said, pacing.

The door opened and Walker came in. He looked extremely confused.

"Uh sir, there's something very strange going on. I just got a call from police in Georgia. They found a red Honda Accord in a lake north of Atlanta. Apparently it was rented by a Mrs. Rebecca Kane of Denver."

Davis stared. "Atlanta? What the hell..."

"Actually, it's near a small town called Acworth. Lake Alatoona. The officer I talked to said that the car has not been there more than an hour."

"Did they find a body?"

"No body. But they do think that two people may have been in the car at some time. The rental company said that a very attractive woman was with Rebecca Kane at the airport when they rented it."

"Donna Houseman?"

146

"I'd say so. Jamie's trying to get the name from United Airlines."

At that moment a young woman walked in and handed Walker a sheet of paper. Walker's eyes glanced over it. He looked up and handed the sheet to the chief. He stared at it for a moment. "Donna Houseman, Rebecca Kane. Flight 701, United, down to Atlanta. This morning!"

"I'd say that settles it," Walker said.

"What the hell were those two women doing in Georgia at some damn lake?" Davis asked no one in particular. Then he sprang into action.

"Jamie, get me on the next plane to Atlanta. Walker, you're coming with me, you're from the south."

"Yes sir," Jamie said and rushed out.

"Got a game plan, sir?" Walker asked.

"There's only one reason for them to be in Georgia. I suddenly remembered that Kane went to Georgia Tech. I'll bet he's there, and called his wife."

"But how did..."

"Who called Rebecca Kane before she left. Do we know that yet?"

"No one, but she herself did call someone."

"Probably Miss Houseman. Walker, we're going to find those women and get some answers. I'll bet you my house that they're not dead."

☠

Wednesday, April 25th, 1994

It was five minutes before eight in the morning when the Boeing 767 landed at Atlanta's Hartsfield airport. As Chief Davis and Walker made their way out, they were met by two policemen. One of them was tall, bearded, and greeted them warmly.

"Welcome to Atlanta, Chief Davis! I'm Chief Larry Williams, Acworth P.D. This is Dale Bidwell, Atlanta P.D."

Davis smiled as the men shook hands. Williams had an extremely strong southern drawl. This was the type of drawl one only hears about. He decided not to waste any time as the men made their way to the parking lot after picking up their baggage.

"Have the bodies been found?"

"No, no bodies," the man named Bidwell said, "We don't think anyone was in the car when it was pushed off into the lake."

"Pushed in to make it look like an accident?"

"Probably. The women are missing, though."

The four men got in a state trooper's car and sped off. Soon, they were heading north on I-75.

"Acworth's about thirty miles up the road," Bidwell said as he drove. "The car was found in a southwest corner of the lake. We think it may be carjacking, or perhaps the women were caught unaware at a gas station..."

"Has the area around the lake been searched?" Davis asked sharply.

Bidwell smiled. "Just because we're southern doesn't make us dumb, chief."

"I didn't say that, but..."

"It's okay, chief," Bidwell said, winking, "We've even got the names of the girls who rented the car."

"Girls?"

"Well... women. Donna Houseman and Rebecca Kane. Their bodies are nowhere to be found."

Davis stared in surprise. "You think there will be bodies?"

148

"Well chief, it's probably a case of carjacking, you know? Some asshole probably bumped into them, and when they stopped and got out, he points a gun at them, takes their car, and probably kills them. It happens all the time in Atlanta."

Davis smiled. "Then this supposed carjacker drives forty miles north and dumps it in a lake?"

"Could happen," Bidwell said, setting his jaw. "You don't know Atlanta, chief. Lots of niggers around here."

"You know, you just contradicted yourself," Davis said calmly.

"Say what?"

"You're southern, and you're dumb. That kind of racist attitude is really not professional demeanor for a policeman."

Bidwell frowned. "That's easy for you to say, chief. You don't try to fight crime in a city of eighty percent blacks."

"You're improving. 'Blacks' is far better," Davis was still the picture of calm.

"Uh let's dump this, gentlemen. We're here I think," Walker broke in.

"We've got a witness," Williams spoke up. "A fisherman named Scott Macey claims he saw a guy dump the car in the lake. He's waiting for you inside."

Davis and Walker were led into the Acworth city police building. Davis had estimated Acworth to be a town of about twenty thousand people. It looked like a typical southern town. He'd always wanted to retire to a town like this one.

They were led into a small interrogation room. Davis noticed that the lighting was very poor. Inside, a tall man with an inordinate amount of facial hair sat at a beat up old desk. He looked intimidated as Davis and Walker walked in, escorted by Bidwell and Williams. Davis looked at the man's shirt pocket, the half open pack of chewing tobacco peering out. He gazed at the man's shifty eyes and greasy fisherman's hat. He knew what Scott Macey was going to be like.

"Mr. Macey, these are policemen from Denver," Williams said, "They'd like to ask you some questions about what you saw."

Macey's eyes narrowed. "Denver? Come a long way, ain't ya?" The man had a thick drawl.

"Mr. Macey, I'm chief Chandler Davis, Denver P.D. I

understand you witnessed a crime."

"I don't know about no crime. I was just fishin' and saw this man drive up in that there car yer after. He gets out, releases the emergency brakes and pushes the car in the lake."

Davis sat down. "Did you get a good look at this man?"

Macey shook his head. "Not a real good look. He was 'bout a hundred feet from me."

"Do the best you can."

"Well let's see. It's like I said to Officer Williams, that man was 'bout six feet or so, normal weight. He wore a blue jacket, though I don't know why. It was damn hot today!"

"Was he a good looking guy?"

Macey looked annoyed. "Hell I don't know. What do you think I am, queer or somethin'?"

"No one's questioning your sexuality, Mr. Macey," Davis said, trying not to sound patronizing, "We're just trying to pinpoint something."

"Did you get a look at his fingers?" Walker asked.

"Fingers? Hell no, I said I was fifty feet away."

"You said hundred," Davis said quickly, "Did this man see you?"

"No. He was worried 'bout somethin'. I figured it was his old lady's car," Macey said, snickering. He showed dirty, irregular shaped teeth as he smiled.

Davis tried to hold his breakfast down, as this man was making him sick. "Did you see anyone in the car, or anyone else around? Maybe a couple of women?"

"Didn't see no wimin."

Davis turned to Bidwell. "I'm through with him. I want to see the car."

Bidwell rose. "It's in the impound. Come with me."

They left Macey and followed Bidwell out to the rear of the building. The impound yard was not impressive. Three cars were parked inside a small tennis-court sized parking lot with a fence around it. Davis looked at the fence and chuckled.

"Don't you think it would be easy for someone to jump over this fence and drive away with their car?"

Bidwell looked at Davis and smirked, "What would they drive away?"

150

Davis looked at the three cars. Bidwell had a point. They were not in the best of shape. The first was an old beat up Grand Prix. The second was a rusty old pickup truck. It was the third car that interested him. It was a late model Honda Accord. He walked up to it. The windows were smashed, and the inside of the car was still wet. He looked inside. There was nothing in the seats.

"We found a cigarette lighter in the car, but that was it," Bidwell said.

This car was driven by a Mrs. Rebecca Kane and a Donna Houseman. Do you have a detailed description of them?" Davis asked.

"Of course, chief," Bidwell said in the same condescending tone, "But you see sir, I don't think we'll find them."

"Why's that?"

"This is rural Georgia, chief. It ain't the big city. There's plenty of places for a person to hide a dead body or two. Ain't you seen Deliverance?"

Davis didn't answer. Instead, he took Walker aside and spoke to him in a low voice.

"These crackers aren't going to help us find jack shit. We need to search ourselves."

"Okay, sir."

Davis turned to face Bidwell. "Well, I think that Officer Walker and I..."

He was interrupted by a policeman who ran into the impound yard. He had a wild look on his face.

"Dale, there's some building on fire out there next to the lake. We need to get out there!"

"Is it Hale barn?" Bidwell asked.

"Think so."

"Let's go," Bidwell said, running towards his car. Davis ran with him.

"What's the big deal? It's just a barn, let the fire department..."

"This barn is next to the lake. It's close to where the car was found," Bidwell cut in, as the four men piled into the car.

"And that is important because?" Davis was still confused.

"What if the bodies are there?"

Davis became more puzzled. "Wasn't this barn searched?"

"Well, we're superstitious about that barn around here. They say some kid died there forty years ago, snooping around."

"Jimmy Randall," Williams added, "He was drunk and fell right on a damn rake. Skewered himself. We don't mess with that barn anymore."

"Are you kidding me!" Davis exploded, "Because of some stupid superstition you're going to ignore proper police procedure and toy with the lives of two women?"

Bidwell was grim as he gripped the steering wheel. "Superstitions mean a lot around here, chief. You bein' from the big city..."

"Bidwell, you're from Atlanta!"

"Never mind that," Bidwell said, "Thing is, since it's burning now, we have no choice but to stop the fire and see if there are any bodies, God bless their souls."

Davis eased back in his seat, thoroughly frustrated. "This is the biggest bunch of horseshit I've ever heard of."

Walker did not speak, but his facial expression indicated that he agreed with the chief.

They were at the burning barn in about ten more minutes. There was already a team of volunteer fire fighters battling the blaze. It was a big barn, sitting quite close to the water. The smoke in the area was thick, blocking out the daylight. Davis jumped out of the car and looked around. The team of firefighters was not large, comprising of about ten men. He decided to help. There was a hose nearby. A firefighter was struggling to hook it up. He ran up to him and helped hook up the hose. The man was wearing a mask, but was clearly grateful. He turned on the water and the two men inched closer to the barn, spraying a deluge of water.

"Is there anyone in there?" Davis yelled.

The firefighter threw up his arms as if to indicate that he did not know. Suddenly he threw down the hose and rushed into the barn through the flaming door. Davis was caught by surprise, but he managed to get the man's clothes nice and wet before he crashed into the barn.

Bidwell was suddenly at his side. "What the hell's he lookin' for? Dead rats?"

"Shut the hell up and help me out here!" Davis screamed,

152

trying to handle his out of control hose.

Bidwell grabbed the end of the hose and the pair went to work. The flames were getting bigger as the whole roof was now on fire. With a loud crash, the left side of the barn caved in, scattering men in all directions.

"Anyone hurt?" someone called out.

"This is useless!" Bidwell screamed at Davis.

Davis did not answer. His mind was on the faceless firefighter that had rushed into the barn. He had not reappeared. Now that he thought about it, something about the man troubled him. He turned to bidwell.

"Where's Walker and Williams?"

"Your boy Walker's over yonder," Bidwell said, nodding his head to the left. "The hell if I know where Williams got to."

Davis spied Walker a few feet to his left. He was also helping out. Another fire truck came rushing into the clearing, and four men leaped out to help. Chaos was settling in.

"Looks like we got all of Acworth out here!" Bidwell said, grinning.

"Someone's coming out the front door!" a voice yelled.

Davis stared. It was the faceless firefighter. As he watched, he noticed that the man was carrying someone on his shoulders. It was a woman. He dropped the hose and ran over to help him, much to Bidwell's chagrin. Another two men rushed over as well.

"Quick! She needs CPR!" the faceless man gasped through his mask. "I'm going back for the other one!"

Davis and the two other men lifted the woman out of the hole that used to be the door and carried her to a safe distance. As they lay her down on the grass, he recognized her. It was Rebecca Kane.

"I know CPR," one of the men said, and started to administer it.

Davis noticed that her pulse was weak. "Damn it, where's the ambulance?"

"That barn's going to collapse soon!" one of the men yelled, "That guy needs to get out of there!"

"She's got a good dose of smoke inhalation," said the man performing CPR, "We need that ambulance!"

"Help!"

Davis whirled around. The faceless man was back at the door. His mask had fallen off. Their eyes met. He ran over to help. The second woman was in his arms. She was also out cold. Davis grabbed her and moved her quickly over to the two men with Rebecca Kane. The faceless man sat down a few yards away, totally exhausted.

"She needs CPR too!" Davis said, gasping. He wished he knew it. He wished he was more in shape too, as this was beginning to drain him. The second man began to administer CPR on her.

Davis turned to look at the faceless firefighter again. He was sitting on the grass, looking at them. His eyes met the chief's again. He smiled wryly at the chief. Davis did not say anything. He knew what he had to do. He called over to Walker, who was also resting now. The barn was now all but lost, and many were trying to put out the remaining fire. Walker rose and came over to him. Davis nodded towards the lone hero. Walker nodded in understanding and went over to the man. A few words were spoken. The two men came over to Davis, and he got up.

"So what now, chief?" the man asked.

An ambulance roared into the clearing, sirens blaring. Two paramedics got out immediately and took control of the situation.

"I'll let you go to the hospital to see them," Davis said. "Walker will escort you. After that, you'll be put under arrest."

The man smiled. "You're all heart, chief."

Davis forced a smile. "I've got a wife too, Kane."

☠

Thursday, April 26th, 1994

It was ten in the morning. The flight from Atlanta back to Denver had just landed at Denver International. It had been a flight of mixed emotions for Mark Kane. It was true that he had saved the women single-handedly. They had been taken to the hospital and released within three hours. Chief Davis had been kind enough to let him have a night with his wife at a hotel, under the watch of local policemen. They had gotten the early flight out of Atlanta today, and were now about to dock at the airport. Mark Kane still felt empty inside. He shuddered as he thought of the millions of questions he would be asked. He had been left alone on the flight, although he was handcuffed and was definitely being treated like a prisoner. His wife and Donna were to take a later flight back. He stared out the plane's window and saw the familiar sights of Denver. A sigh escaped his mouth.

Chief Davis got up to get his luggage as the plane stopped. Kane got up along with Detective Walker, who was his escort. A fleeting thought entered his mind. Should he try to escape when they were in the airport? He thought for a second and decided against it. He was tired of running. He'd sit and try a more rational approach to the whole situation.

They disembarked from the plane and strode out into the customs area. They went to baggage claim and quickly gathered their luggage. All the time, no one spoke to Kane. As they were coming out, Kane spotted the bar. This was the place. That man ... who was he? He looked in and tried to spot the bartender. It was not the same black man, but an old woman there instead. The bar was deserted as usual. Kane wondered how they ever did any business.

The trio got into a waiting police car. They started their twenty-five minute drive to metropolitan police. Kane said nothing to anyone. He knew that he had better save his breath, as there would be many questions. He stared out the car window and wondered if he would be allowed a phone call. Who would he call? Wellington? After his stunt, he would not be surprised if Wellington had dropped his case. Maybe he'd call Donald Watts. Watts had always been interested in his case a lot more than Wellington. Unfortunately, Watts was a prosecutor. A smile came to his face. Of course! He knew whom he'd call.

When they arrived at the precinct, Kane turned to Chief Davis.

"Chief, can I make a quick phone call?"

The chief nodded. Walker led him to a phone. He picked up and dialed a familiar number. A woman answered.

"Hello. Kane residence."

"Nadine? How are you?" Kane's voice was soft.

"Mark? Is that you? Where have you been?"

"I've been away, thinking," Kane said, "Are the kids in?"

"The kids are at school, Mark. I'm watching them while Becky is away. Is she with you?"

"No, they'll be back later today Nadine. Tell the kids that I'll see them soon, okay?"

"Where are you? When are you coming back?"

"I'm at the police station. I'll be back as soon as I can," Kane said sadly.

"I'll have Becky come by there when she gets back," Nadine said. "Mark, you hang in there."

"I don't think you'll have to do that. I have a feeling she'll come here before she gets home."

Kane hung up and was led by Walker directly to a cell. He had figured on the chief questioning him before this, but this was apparently not going to be the case.

"Chief'll see you tomorrow. You'll not be allowed any visitors today," Walker said in a stone cold voice. He shut the cell shut and left.

Kane looked around and sighed. He had seen this cell before. It was a holding cell. He sat down and leaned his head against the wall. It was time for him to think.

It was after lunch when Rebecca Kane walked into the office of Chief Davis. She did not look happy. The chief saw her and held up his hands to thwart anything she might say. It did not work.

156

"Chief, I demand that you let my husband go. He saved both me and Miss Houseman from sure death."

Davis shook his head firmly. "Mrs. Kane, I can't do that. Your husband is now under arrest for the murder of four people. He is also charged with assault on Mr. David Lemming, and skipping town. As much as I hate to tell you this, your husband really made things look bad for himself with these stunts."

Rebecca Kane sat down. "Surely you don't think that he committed those murders?"

"It doesn't matter any more what I think, Mrs. Kane," Davis said calmly, "Things simply look very bad for him."

"What about the fact that he saved us? Doesn't that count for something?"

Davis sat down and faced the irate Mrs. Kane. "So he saved two women who are very dear to him. That's great. That still doesn't excuse him from the other..."

"Damn it, he didn't commit those murders!"

Davis decided to go on the offensive. "Mrs. Kane, what were you and Miss Houseman doing in Georgia anyway? How did you know he was there?"

Rebecca Kane Bit her lip. "Well, we didn't really know. Donna guessed."

Davis raised his eyebrows. "She guessed?"

"It was an educated guess. They had known each other in college, and that particular barn was very special to them. So on a hunch, we went to try and find him."

Davis leaned back in his chair. "I see. And what were you going to do with him once you found him?"

"I don't know. It turned out that we didn't find him. We went into the barn and were locked in from the outside by someone. Pretty soon I heard the car get started and driven off."

"You have no idea who this person was?"

Rebecca Kane shook her head. "Not a clue. Anyway, we decided to just sit there and wait, because there was no way we were going to break down that door. We went to sleep, and the next thing I know is waking up in the hospital."

Davis was silent for a moment. Then he got up. "I suppose you want to see your husband."

"You suppose correctly."

Davis led her down to visitation. Rebecca had to wait a couple of minutes before Mark was brought out. She stared at him. He had dark circles under his eyes, and looked like he was sick.

"Honey, what happened to you?" she asked, sitting down beside him.

Mark managed a wan smile. "I'm okay. How are you and the kids holding up?"

"Well, under the circumstances. Mark, we're going to get you out of here."

Mark Kane sighed. "Becky hon, it looks pretty bad for me. I think I screwed it all up by going to Georgia."

"I wish we hadn't gone after you. They probably wouldn't have found you then."

Mark stroked his wife's hair. "You're wrong there. Remember, we weren't alone. Whoever tried to kill you two knew I was there."

"I'll talk to Phil Wellington. Maybe he..."

"Dump Phil," Mark said, "Get a hold of Donald Watts. He impresses me a hell of a lot more."

"Donald Watts? He's a prosecutor!"

Mark smiled. "I don't want him for a lawyer. I want him to investigate this further. I don't think he believes I'm guilty."

"You know what we have to do?" Rebecca Kane said, "We have to find that man. That man, John Kirby. He's the guy we need to get a hold of. He's..."

"Yes, Kirby," Kane said, a frown on his face. "That guy's the whole key."

Upstairs, Chief Davis was having a similar conversation with Detective Walker.

"I called Mr. Lemming, sir. He said he'd be over shortly."

Davis motioned Walker to sit down. "Let's talk for a sec bud."

Walker sat down. He was always somewhat nervous around his boss. He was just that type of person.

Davis looked up at the ceiling and spoke. "What's new on Blackwood?"

"Not a thing, sir."

"What about Kirby?"

"Can't find him anywhere."

Davis frowned. "This Kirby fellow troubles me. He's got six fingers, he's non descript, average looking, shows up at an airport muttering some horseshit about women, shows up at the Kelly murder according to Lemming, etcetera, etcetera. This guy is incredibly involved in the case, and yet I've never met him. This guy has six fingers..."

Walker didn't say anything as Davis trailed off, deep in thought. He knew not to interrupt him when he was thinking.

Davis looked at Walker now. "Do you suppose an engineer could have enemies? From someone at work, maybe?"

Walker coughed. "I suppose it's possible, sir."

"Suppose someone he deals with, not from work, but maybe a supplier, gets pissed off at him? He is a design engineer, he has to deal with many vendors."

Walker smiled. "Sir, I doubt a whole company would..."

Davis held up his hand. "What if a singular person who owns a company has all his eggs in KBATech? Suppose KBATech drops him. Suppose that decision is made by Kane. Would that maybe make him an enemy?"

"Sir, I'm not quite sure what you're getting at. I thought you were quite sure that it was Kane."

"Of course, it's Kane. I know it had to be Kane," Davis said, "But humor me, will you? Check out a person named Roy Drake."

Walker realized that he'd been had. "You've already done some research, haven't you sir?"

Davis smiled and winked. "Leave no stone unturned, Matt. You never know where you'll find maggots."

Walker groaned and left the room, leaving Davis to smile contently.

David Lemming walked into the chief's office with a grin on his face. Davis looked at him as he strode in. The man had an air of confidence about him.

"You got our fish back from the peach state, huh? Where is he, I have to talk to him."

Davis smiled. "Sit down Mr. Lemming. Before you talk to him, I have a few things that may interest you."

159

Lemming appeared curious enough, Davis thought. He quickly sat down with a questioning look on his face.

"First of all, how did you know he was in Georgia?"

Lemming smiled. "I know a lot more than you think."

Davis folded his arms. "Really? Well, do you know about a man named Roy Drake?"

Lemming's eyes narrowed. "Roy Drake?"

"So you haven't been as thorough as you would have thought," Davis said with great satisfaction. "Roy Drake is a salesman. Actually, he's the owner of American Tube, right here in Denver. He supplied KBATech with most of their copper tubing and other copper and copper alloy materials. They use a lot of the stuff."

Lemming said nothing. Davis continued.

"Let's just say, for business reasons, American Tube was bumped by KBATech. Our friend Kane was the project engineer who dealt directly with Drake, but he wasn't the man who made the decision to dump the company. It was their president who did it, and that was unknown to Kane."

Lemming smiled. "Is there a point here?"

"Suppose Mr. Roy Drake is dealt such a financial setback by this shaft up the rear end that he decides to get revenge on the person he believes screwed him. Suppose he follows this person to a bar at the airport that same day and disguises himself as an ordinary looking man. Now suppose he strikes up a conversation with this person about women and other general bullshit?"

Lemming looked skeptical. "Are you suggesting..."

"I'm not suggesting anything," Davis said, "It's a theory. You must admit that it's a plausible alternative. You see, this whole John Kirby thing has puzzled me from the beginning. This man is just too fake to be true. Six fingers? One time he's ordinary looking, non-descript. You met the man. Was he non-descript?"

Lemming frowned. "No, actually he was a fairly good looking fellow. But he could have worn a disguise. As you said, I did meet him."

"Yes you did," Davis said thoughtfully, "But did you meet the real John Kirby?"

"Well, the guy was nervous, and he did lie about who he was, that much I am sure of. He said he was a cousin, and Virginia

160

Kelly doesn't have a cousin by the name of John Kirby. So I just figured he lied about being her cousin."

Davis leaned forward. "But who was he? If he wasn't her cousin, why was he there? Was he our mysterious airport bar John Kirby in the flesh without a disguise? Funny how that name pops up everywhere you look."

Lemming fidgeted in his chair. "I don't think the man I saw was in disguise."

"No, he wasn't," Davis said, "And his name wasn't John Kirby. I give you this to ponder, Mr. Lemming. I say to you that John Kirby doesn't exist. He's a figment of someone's imagination."

"Whose imagination?"

"The killer's imagination, of course."

"You're saying Kane whipped him out of thin air as a smokescreen?" Lemming was incredulous.

Davis frowned. "I'm not sure. I'm not sure how Kane fits into this whole thing. He's involved somehow, but it's still a puzzle."

Lemming shook his head. "But chief, I met the guy. And what about Kane's antics in Georgia?"

"Let's ask him," Davis said, pressing a button on his desk. "Walker, bring Kane in here please."

In a few minutes, Mark Kane was marched into the office by Detective Walker. At the sight of Lemming, he looked nervous.

"Pull up a seat, Kane," Davis said with a smile. "Walker, you stay."

Kane did as instructed, looking at Lemming warily. Lemming gave him a reassuring smile.

"Did you see you wife?" he asked.

Kane nodded.

"She's a lovely woman, Mr. Kane. You're very lucky."

"Yes I am."

Davis lit a cigarette. He took one puff and looked at Kane in a businesslike manner.

"Mr. Kane, let's just get to the point. You assaulted Mr. Lemming here a few days ago and fled to Georgia, am I correct?"

Kane smiled wryly. "In a nutshell, you're right."

"Good," Davis said and leaned back in his chair, arms

behind his head. "Now tell me, why did you do that?"

"The truth?"

"The truth would be nice."

"Well, I felt cornered. I didn't kill that woman, but it looked real bad, the way Mr. Lemming found me. I had to act fast, so I picked up a solid object and hit Mr. Lemming on the head, hard enough to knock him out. I'm sorry I had to resort to that."

Lemming rubbed his head. "So am I."

Davis smiled. "What did you do then?"

"I got in my car and drove around for a while, totally panicky. I then decided to go to Georgia to get away and think about things for a little while, so I got on a plane, under an assumed name."

Davis's smile got wider. "What assumed name did you use?"

Kane forced a grin. "John Kirby. Don't ask me why."

Davis nodded. "I know why. You're not used to assumed names, so you picked the one that came into your head. Funny how that name keeps floating around."

Kane continued, "Anyway, after I got to Atlanta, I rented a car and went to the barn by the lake. I stayed there for a little while, until I noticed a day or two later that I was going to have company."

"Your wife and Miss Houseman?"

"Yes, and they were going to the barn. I decided to hide. They looked around for a while, and then left. I really didn't want for them to find me. I was going to settle in for the night when I heard them coming again. I left hastily, and hid out. I saw someone come to the door and lock them in. He then stole their car and drove away. I wanted to let them out, but I didn't want to be found. I figured that they'd be safe locked in, so I left and slept under a tree in the woods. The next day I woke up to smell smoke and fire, and rushed down to see the barn in flames. You know the rest of the story."

Davis nodded. "You didn't get a look at this person who locked them in?"

Kane looked down. "No, I didn't. It was getting dark, and I was a good distance away. I am pretty sure it was a man, though."

"Could you have been followed by anyone after you left the

Brown apartment?" Davis asked.

Kane shook his head. "To tell you the truth, if I had been followed, I wouldn't have noticed. My mind was thinking of a hundred different things."

Davis leaned forward again. "I'm going to switch gears on you," he said. "Do you know a man named Roy Drake?"

Kane looked surprised. "Yeah, I know Roy. Why?"

"Did you recently drop his company, American Tube, as a supplier to KBATech?"

Kane was taken aback. "Well I didn't personally, but yes, KBATech did. We're a growing company, and we've recently merged with a large corporation. We decided to go with a company with a more nineties approach to manufacturing. You know, ISO9000 certification and all that. I hated that we had to do that to Roy, but really he shouldn't depend on one company so much. His company's a little behind the times. They don't even do a four sigma on their control charts, can you believe that? In today's manufacturing, one needs..."

Davis held up his hand. "I don't need a lecture on manufacturing engineering, Mr. Kane. My point is this. How well do you know Mr. Drake? Would he be prone to perhaps seek revenge on you?"

Kane looked shocked. "You're not seriously going to say that Roy Drake is behind all this?"

"You have to consider all possibilities, no matter how remote they may seem," Davis said.

Lemming spoke up. "This man you met at the bar at the airport. Did he have six fingers?"

"Six fingers? No, I don't think so. I would have noticed that."

"The bartender said he did," Lemming stated.

Kane shook his head. "No way. I took special note of the man's appearance. He didn't have anything out of the ordinary about him. I did get the feeling I have seen him before, though. He's familiar, yet he isn't."

"Getting back to Roy Drake," Davis said, annoyed at the subject change, "I am having him looked into. Walker, anything so far?"

"Nothing out of the ordinary, sir. We're still digging,

163

though."

"Is Blackwood still missing?" Lemming asked.

Walker nodded. "Yes he is."

Lemming frowned. "Blackwood worries me. Why is he missing? I have a feeling..."

"Let me tell you what I think," Davis interrupted, "I think that the man you saw at the Virginia Kelly murder was Robert Blackwood. I just realized that you've never met Blackwood, Mr. Lemming. I wish I had a picture of the guy."

"That makes sense," Lemming said. "He also fits the personality of the man that Kane here met at the bar."

Kane looked at Chief Davis. "Chief, this is all well and good, but what's my status? You come up here and question me, and I get the feeling that you still don't think I did it. Yet I'm still under arrest for murder."

"Kane, I didn't say that I bought your story," Davis said coldly. "As far as I know, you may have killed every single one of these people. I'm just trying to weed out the alternatives."

"I see," Kane said quietly.

Lemming looked at his watch. "Chief, I hate to leave, but I have to meet someone. Please keep me updated."

"I will," Davis said, as Lemming strode out. He looked at Kane. The man had a decidedly rough look to him today. It was probably lack of sleep.

"I guess we'll sit around for your lawyer now," he said.

"Donald Watts?"

"Yes, he called earlier. He said that he had some important info to share with us."

Kane brightened. "That man's sharp. If he can't help, no one can."

Davis did not smile. "Are you sure you want to hear what he has to say, Kane?"

Kane did not answer.

Rebecca Kane sat down on her living room sofa with a glass of soda in her hand and looked at the woman on the adjacent couch. Donna Houseman was sitting there, biting her nails.

"That's a terrible habit you know," she said, taking a sip of her drink.

"Can't help it," Donna said, "I wish the chief would call with some news."

"I'm going to visit Mark again later," Rebecca said.

Donna stared at the mock Van Gogh on the wall. "Do you suppose there's any chance they'll find that Blackwood character? He did all this shit, you know."

"You're sure?"

Donna stared at Rebecca. "Well, it certainly wasn't Mark!"

Rebecca Kane did not say anything. She'd known Mark for a long time, and there was just no way in her mind that he could commit a murder. Still, how much do people actually know about each other? She shook away the doubts in her head as quickly as they had crept in.

"No, no, you're right, it wasn't Mark."

She flicked on the television. The bald head of Montel Williams flashed, and soon they were embarking on an adventure with teenage mothers who wanted to give up their children for adoption. The two women snickered as idiot after idiot yelled back and forth at each other. The shouting match continued as one mother revealed that she was not only going to give up her baby for adoption, but wanted to have another baby and give it up as well. The human drama distracted the women enough that they did not notice the small Ford Escort that pulled in the driveway. A middle-aged woman got out and rushed to their door.

Inside the house, Donna got up to get herself a drink. As she did, there was a loud knocking at the door.

"I'll get it," she announced and strode towards the door. She looked through the peephole and saw a middle-aged woman. She looked to be anxious. She opened the door.

The woman barged into the house as soon as the door was opened. "Ok, where is he? I know he's in here!"

Donna stared at her in surprise. Rebecca got up from the sofa and reached for her gun. It wasn't where she usually kept it. She turned toward the strange woman.

"Excuse me?"

"Where is he?" The woman was frantic. She resembled a woman scorned in the worst way.

"Um, ma'am, who are you, and what do you want?" Rebecca asked.

The woman looked disgusted. "Two women. Some people have no shame!"

Donna stepped forward. "Look, I'm going to have to call the police if you don't tell us who you are and what you're doing here."

The woman licked her lips in nervous tension. Rebecca Kane tried to size her up for future purposes. She was about five foot four, weighed about a hundred and thirty pounds. She looked to be about forty, and was not particularly attractive. Her nose was a mile long, and she certainly did not know how to dress. Her cheap pumps gave the impression of the stereotype penny pincher. She did wear a wedding ring.

"I'm going to repeat. Who are you?" Donna stepped forward another step.

"Don't pretend he's not here!" The woman was getting hysterical. "His car's parked right in front of the house. He's cheated on me once too many times!"

Rebecca Kane was starting to get fed up. "Look, Miss whoever you are, my friend is going to call the police and have you arrested for trespassing. Donna, please call Chief Davis."

"Take a look! His car's right outside!"

Donna picked up the phone. "Whose car?"

"My car," a man's voice came from the kitchen entrance. She whirled around to face the voice. There was indeed a man standing there. He was brandishing a gun.

"You ladies really shouldn't leave your guns lying about. Makes it really easy for someone to come in and do what I am about to do." The man was smiling calmly.

Rebecca Kane stepped forward. The man waved his gun. "No no, my dear lady. You sit down. And Miss Houseman, please put down that phone. It won't do you any good, the line is dead. I took the liberty of cutting it."

Donna put down the phone and sat down. The strange woman also sat down, surprisingly quiet in her demeanor.

"Joyce, I do hate to disillusion you, but I'm not cheating on you," the man said, grinning. "Although I wouldn't mind doing it with these women here."

"You're disgusting!" the woman referred to as "Joyce" screamed.

The man waved his gun. "Now Joyce, you're not going to tarnish my reputation, so I have to figure out what I'm going to do with you three women. Maybe I'll have to tie you all up and throw you in another burning barn."

"It was you!" Donna said angrily.

"Yes, it was me," the man said, turning on the overhead light. Now they could see him clearly. "However, that failed, due to the surprising heroics by your foolish husband, Mrs. Kane. This time, I'll have to do a better job."

"Somehow, this doesn't surprise me all that much," Rebecca Kane said.

The man turned to face her. "Doesn't it, Mrs. Kane? I didn't think it would. You're quite a smart woman. Attractive too, I might add."

"I can't tell you how little your compliments mean to me," Rebecca Kane retorted.

"Feisty, too," the man said. "No matter. It's time to go. Come on, everyone get into the car. Miss Houseman, you do the driving. I'll sit in the back with Joyce."

Kane stared at the walls of Chief Davis's office. It was starting to get late on in the afternoon. He wondered why Rebecca had not visited yet. Chief Davis was off doing something, but he had said that he would be "right back." That was about half an hour ago. Now here he sat with the expressionless Matthew Walker, who had the personality of a paperweight.

"You know, I'm innocent," he said, deciding to prod on the detective.

Walker said nothing. He appeared to be nodding off. What a flunky he was, Kane thought. He started to think about the possibility of Roy Drake. The more he thought about it, the more it made sense to him. What if he was indeed the type of person who was calculating and vengeful. He could see Roy pulling a stunt like that. Then his thoughts were blocked by a problem. How did the Kelly murder figure in then? Did it figure in at all? Did Roy Drake in fact copy that particular crime?

Kane stared at the now sleeping Matt Walker. He could probably walk out of here right now and make his escape. He decided against it. He would probably be caught again, making him look guiltier.

As he looked at the door, Chief Davis came back in. He had an odd look on his face.

"What's up?"

Donald Watts came into the room right behind the chief. He looked at Kane and smiled. Kane smiled back. Both men sat down. Davis was still deep in thought. Watts looked at Kane and spoke up.

"Mr. Kane, it's nice to see you. Interesting case you're wrapped up in."

"I wish it was less interesting and much clearer."

Watts grinned. "Maybe I can help some. I have been following this case, out of pure curiosity. Chief Davis has filled me in on some of the details, and I agree with him on one thing. John Kirby is a bogus name. He doesn't exist."

Kane grimaced. "Tell me that's not all you have."

Watts studied Kane's face carefully. "What about this then? The John Kirby that David Lemming met at the Virginia Kelly murder site is a totally different person than the one you met. The one you met is the killer. The one Mr. Lemming met was the one who came up with the fictitious name, though."

"How do you figure that?" Kane asked.

"I don't," Watts said and turned to the chief. "Chief, you want to call him in?"

"Mr. Love, please come in," Davis called out.

The door opened, and Tyrone Love the bartender came in. He did not look very pleased to be there. He slumped down into a chair.

Davis got up and faced Kane. "Mr. Love here will, for your benefit Mr. Kane, answer a few questions for us," he said with a nasty smile on his face. He turned to the large bartender.

"Mr. Love, do you recognize this man?" he pointed to Kane.

Tyrone Love looked at Kane with little interest. "Yeah, he's the guy at the bar."

"The guy at the bar," Davis echoed, "Which guy is that?"

Love sighed. "The guy who walked in that day and had the strange conversation with that strange man about women and shit."

Davis stared at Love. "You said that this other man had

168

what? Six fingers, am I not right?"

Love looked uncomfortable. "Look chief, I..."

"Now I want the truth," Davis interrupted, "Did the other man have six fingers or not? Don't lie to me Mr. Love, I already know the truth."

Love looked beaten. "No, he didn't. I made that up because I couldn't remember what he looked like. I wanted to sort of sensationalize the story, hoping it would be picked up by the media."

"It would have been, had I released this bit of information to the public," Davis said sternly. "Luckily, I kept in under strict wraps. It's a good thing, for if I had not, I would be looking like the biggest ass in the world right now."

Kane was thunderstruck. "You made up this bullshit, knowing a man's life hangs in the balance? You should be horsewhipped."

Love hung his head. "Look, I'm sorry. I don't know what else to say."

Watts reached into his shirt pocket and pulled something out. "Lucky for you I have a picture." He showed it to the hapless bartender. "Does this ring a bell?"

Tyrone Love looked at the picture and immediately shook his head. "That's not him. This guy's too young looking, too healthy, and too dark."

Davis looked at the picture. "That is a picture of Mr. Robert Blackwood. As of right now, he is missing."

Kane stared at the picture. "You're right, Mr. Watts. This guy was not the guy at the bar. No amount of disguise could change him to that guy."

Davis picked up the phone and dialed a number. "I'm going to call Lemming and get his ass over here. Maybe he can tell us if Blackwood was the guy he saw at the Kelly murder site. Hope he's home."

The phone was picked up on the third ring. It was answered by a young man's voice. Davis put it on the speakerphone.

"Hello."

"Mr. David Lemming, please."

"I'm sorry, he's not here."

"I see. Could you leave him a message for me? I guess

you're the Harvard boy, huh?" Davis was smiling as he spoke.

"Excuse me?"

"Harvard. You're his son, right?"

"His son? Harvard? What are you talking about?"

Davis frowned. "I'm sorry, I mistook you for his son. Who is this?"

"This is his nephew Jeff. He doesn't have a son. He has a daughter. She's only eight, and certainly can't attend Harvard. Who is this anyway?"

Davis exchanged perplexed glances with Kane and Watts. "Never mind son. We'll call him back."

He hung up and looked at the floor in a funny manner.

"That's strange," Kane stated. "I was under the impression that his son was going to Harvard too. Guess he was pulling our chain."

Davis looked up. He had a gleam in his eyes. "Guys, suppose Donald is right. Suppose the two John Kirby's are that. Two different people. If that is so, who is the only person that the second John Kirby can be? The one that was at the airport bar?"

Kane struggled to comprehend. "Well, I guess..."

"No guessing required. It could only be the person who had heard the name "John Kirby" mentioned before as a fictitious name. This person in a bit of brilliance decides to give the same fictitious name to Kane at the bar. All falls into place. This bogus John Kirby will be blamed for the whole thing if the frame-up job on Kane doesn't work."

Kane frowned. "But the only other time the name was used was in the Kelly murder. The bogus John Kirby gave his name to David..."

"...Lemming," Davis finished. He smiled, as if to let the meaning of this sink in.

"Lemming?" Watts had a puzzled look on his face.

"Yes, Lemming. It all makes sense. He's the only one who has heard the name used before," Davis said triumphantly. "That little revelation about his non-existent son makes sense now, too. I always wondered why Lemming drove such a shitty car. He couldn't afford it because he had been paying someone blackmail money. A lot of blackmail money, for a long time. He made up a story about a Harvard son, knowing we'd never check that up."

"Then other things make sense too," Kane said, suddenly energized, "He must have set me up for the murder of Teresa Brown. I'll bet he's the one who came down to Georgia and tried to kill Becky and Donna. No wonder he tried to spook me with that letter from the Kelly girl."

"I'll be willing to bet that he was shelling out big bucks to Teresa Brown and Travis Singeton as well, and that's why he had to kill them," Davis said, still triumphant.

Watts was grave. "This makes sense, but why would he kill the two girls?"

"That we have to find out," Davis said, getting his gun, "Let's go."

"Where are we going to go?" Kane asked.

Davis stopped. "That's right, you can't go. You're just being questioned. You should be in jail."

Kane threw up his hands. "Didn't we just determine that I'm innocent?"

Davis took a long look at Kane. "All right, you can come with us. If you're involved in any way, so help you God..."

Kane smiled. "Trust me chief, I'm not!"

"Ok, let's go then. We'll go to Lemming's house. There may be a clue there as to where he went. He might even get there by the time we do."

The three men piled into Davis's cruiser and they sped off. Kane settled into his chair, his spirits both lifted and curious. He was dying to know why a reputed detective would commit multiple murders. The more he thought, the more things fell into place. He pictured the man at the bar. He pictured David Lemming with a toupee. Yes, it was him all right. He knew that he looked familiar. He tried to piece together the devious plan Lemming had. He couldn't do it. He needed more facts.

Three pairs of eyes looked up at the man before them. None of the three women they belonged to could say much. They were all gagged and tied to a tree. The man who had done this to them was about fifty feet away, digging some sort of ditch. There was still some daylight, but night was approaching. The man worked at a fast pace, shoveling dirt away in big chunks with a large shovel. He smiled as he did all of this. The smile was not a pleasant one.

"Sorry I had to drag you girls into this, but you can blame my wife Joyce. She's the reason behind it all. Ask her!" he said angrily. Then he laughed insanely. "I'm sorry! You can't ask her, can you! You're bound and gagged!"

Rebecca Kane tried to say something. He noticed this, and came walking over to her, shovel still in his hand.

"What's that honey? You want to say something?"

Rebecca mumbled. The man laughed hysterically. Then his face turned serious. "It's really too bad you know. I really got into this because of fear, fear of my wife taking everything from me. Now it looks like I have to take everything from her. You two were just in the way."

Donna Houseman tried to open her mouth to scream. A gurgling noise came out through her gag. It was on extremely tight.

"Trying to attract attention?" the man said, grinning nastily, "Go ahead! You're in the boonies hon!"

He went back to his ditch and started digging. "That reminds me of a philosophical question," he said, "If three women scream in the woods and there's no one there, do they make a noise?"

He laughed again. "What do you think of that, huh? Socrates, Plato, eat your heart out!"

Rebecca Kane tried to bite through her gag. It was no use. After futile efforts that only resulted in wasting energy, she gave up on it. She leaned back against the large tree, hoping against hope that some hikers would come along. Then she realized that hikers would be no match for a man with a gun. A desperate man with a gun, at that. She looked at the figure of David Lemming with distaste, trying to figure out what was going on. She knew one thing for sure. Lemming was the murderer, and that somehow her husband was framed by the man. How or why she did not know, nor could she begin to guess. She shuddered, as the evening was beginning to get cold.

Slowly her thoughts drifted to her husband. He was right now in jail, and had no idea what was happening. She saw no way that the police would realize the truth. She closed her eyes, as a teardrop fell to the ground. No! She had to be strong! There was still hope. She must try and think of a means of escape. She nudged Donna with her shoulder. Donna tried to look at her, but it was awkward. She tried to convey a message to her with her eyes. Would Donna understand her indication to try and think of an escape? She apparently did, because she winked at her. Her hopes went up. Donna Houseman was a clever woman. She would think of a way out of this mess. Her thoughts were dashed, though, when Donna's head drooped. She had gone to sleep. The poor woman was dead tired.

"You know girls, just in case you think I haven't thought this through I'll tell you something," Lemming said, stopping his digging for a moment. "You three will go down as victims of a blazing car accident. They won't even bother to find your bodies, it will be so bad. Of course, I'll find clues to lead the police in that path."

Rebecca's heart sank. The man was a monster, and everything he said would work! He had a great reputation in the Denver community. No one would ever suspect him. She wondered why such a prominent detective would commit such grisly murders. She guessed it was either a crime of passion or money. She tried to deduce. What had he said? He did this all because of fear? Fear of losing money to his wife? He must have done something that would have enabled her to take his money. No wonder he drove such a beat up old car. All of his money must have been tied up in payoffs.

She felt a kick at her knees. Turning her head carefully, she saw Joyce trying to get her attention. She was trying to nod her head in a direction. She followed her head nod. She seemed to be nodding towards a clump of trees to her right. Oh how she wished it wasn't getting dark. It was twilight now, but she couldn't see what Joyce Lemming was trying to get at. She shook her head to indicate to her that she didn't see anything. Joyce closed her eyes and looked skyward.

She didn't know when she had nodded off to sleep, but she was shaken awake by David Lemming in what seemed to be a few minutes. She blinked. It was dark now, and Lemming held a flashlight.

"Let's go honey, it's your turn."

Rebecca looked around her. She was still tied to the tree, but she couldn't see the other two women. Alarms went off in her head. She struggled as Lemming cut her ropes. He was holding the

173

gun still, so she dared not do much more.

"Are you thirsty?" Lemming asked.

She nodded vigorously as the last rope was cut. She felt the tension ease and let out a gasp through her gag. Lemming smiled and brought out a can of coke from a bag.

"Can't say I let a lady go thirsty," he said, undoing her gag. She took a big sip of the coke and drank it. Then she took another sip and spit it at Lemming's face.

"That wasn't very smart, Mrs. Kane," he said angrily.

"Fuck you," Rebecca hissed.

"Oh that's nice. In thirty years we've gone from "Ask not what your country can do for you" to "Fuck you". The media's right. We are going downhill as a nation."

"Nice to meet you Mr. Pot," Rebecca said, "And by the way, why do you call Mr. Kettle black, anyway?"

Lemming smiled. "I'm going to miss you most. You're quite the spitfire."

"Thank you, but I really don't give a shit who or what you're going to miss. I want you to let me and my friends go right now."

Lemming grinned. "Let you go? Let me think... No, I don't think I can do that. You see, I consider you three to know too much. And me, I'm a selfish guy. I only think of myself, and thus I can't let you go."

"You'll be caught you know. They'll catch on to you sooner or later."

Lemming's grin disappeared. "You think so? How will they do that? Educate me, will you Mrs. Kane?"

Rebecca sighed. "My husband is smart. So is the chief." She immediately hated that answer. It didn't sound very convincing at all. Still, maybe she was buying time.

Lemming rubbed his hands together. "Yes, they're very smart. That's why they're still trying to track down that idiot Blackwood and chasing wild geese after people named John Kirby."

Rebecca didn't have much else to say, but she had to stall.

"Uh, Mr. Lemming, tell me why you committed these murders," she said slowly.

Kane whistled. "No my dear, that's a story I'll take to my

174

grave, and so will you, literally."

"You're going to kill me anyway. Why not grant me that wish?"

Lemming grinned again and moved his face closer to hers. His lips brushed her ears as he whispered.

"Because in movies, granting people last wishes always comes back to haunt the villain."

He got up and waved his gun. He took the ropes and tied her hands together and ordered her to start walking. She did so, with him following behind.

"At least tell me how you thought of this clever plan to frame my husband."

Lemming stopped and turned around slowly. The grin was still on his face.

"What's that? Now you're trying to butter me up? My dear lady, don't try to play mind games with the master."

"You're the master of mind games?" Rebecca laughed.

Lemming was not pleased with her amusement. "You think that's funny? Well honey, you're on the losing end, aren't you? Now march!"

The Race is On

Chief Davis's cruiser pulled into the driveway of David Lemming's residence noisily. The three men jumped out and rushed to the front door. Kane noticed that there were no cars parked in the driveway. Davis and Watts both pulled their guns as he knocked on the door. It was opened almost immediately by a red headed boy who looked to be in his mid-teens.

"Hello son," Davis greeted. "Could we speak to David please? Just call him out here."

"Uncle David's not here," the boy said, a little wide-eyed. "What's going on?"

Davis smiled. "Well, do you know where he is?"

"No sir. I'm just stayin' here for a few days. He's hardly ever here. Auntie was here, but she got mad and ran off somewhere too."

"Auntie?" Davis asked, "Is this your Uncle David's wife?"

The boy made a face. "Of course, what do you think?"

"Where did your aunt run off to?" Kane asked.

The boy shrugged. "I don't know. She was on the phone, and the next thing I know she got mad and rushed off, muttering something to herself. I think she's going a little crazy lately, if you ask me."

Davis went inside the house and examined the table where the phone was located. There was a rolodex there, and it was open. The card it was open to had a name and number on it.

"Steven Pace, P.I.," he echoed. Turning to Walker, he asked if the name was familiar to him.

"Pace is a detective. I think he specializes in spying on husbands and wives," Walker answered.

"That figures," Davis said, dialing the number on the card quickly. It was answered by a machine.

"Hi, this is Steven Pace. I'm not in the office right now. If this is an emergency, page me at 555-3890. This can be..."

176

Davis hung up and immediately dialed the number. The other men walked over to him. Davis hung up.

"Well, that's paged him. Let's hope he calls back quickly."

Kane had a frown on his face. "Uh chief, exactly what is this going to solve?"

Davis sighed. "Kane, we're looking for Lemming. His wife was on the phone, probably with this dick Pace, who is an adulterer chaser. She gets off the phone, and storms out of the house. Chances are pretty good that she's caught Lemming cheating on her, thanks to Pace, who knows where he is."

Kane whistled. "Damn, that's good. You are supposing that she went to try and find him."

Davis smiled. "Kane, detective work is eighty percent guesswork. Educated guesswork, but still guesswork. I remember the time..."

He was interrupted by the phone ringing. He snatched it up. "Hello."

"Pace here. Who's this?"

"Mr. Pace, this is chief Chandler Davis, Denver P.D. I have a few questions to ask you."

"Can you hurry it up? I'm in the middle of a juicy one."

"Does it involve murder?" Davis asked innocently.

"Well no, but..."

"Then shut the hell up and listen!" Davis yelled. "You have a client named..." he paused, realizing that he didn't know Lemming's wife's name. He looked at the boy questioningly.

"Joyce," the boy mouthed.

"...Joyce Lemming. I need to know about your conversation with her earlier today."

Pace was suspicious. "Listen, I can't give you that information. How do I know you're the police chief, anyway. You could be..."

"I don't have time for this shit!" Davis was furious, "Every second we waste, he may be getting away."

"Who's getting away?"

"The man you've been tailing. David Lemming."

"Oh him," Pace laughed,"He was easy to find. He was holed up at some woman's house on Clayton drive. Followed him right to the place."

"Give me an address," Davis asked tensely.

"All right, all right," Pace said in mock disgust, "It's 2114 Clayton drive. Are you happy?"

"Ecstatic. Thank you Mr. Pace, you've been a big help."

Davis hung up and looked at the others. "2114 Clayton drive," he said grimly.

Kane's face showed horror. "That's my house!"

Davis nodded. "Exactly."

The next few hours were a blur. The four men piled back into the cruiser and headed to Kane's house. The sky was darkening now, as the night was settling in. It took about twenty minutes to get to the house, with the sirens blaring. The men did not speak one word to each other on the trip. Intensity was on their faces. Kane was the picture of grim tension. They pulled into Kane's driveway with a screeching halt. The men got out and stared at the three cars parked outside.

"Donna's car is here, Becky's car is here," Kane observed, "I don't know who this escort belongs to."

Davis rushed over to the door, gun drawn. He flung himself against the side and rang the doorbell. The other men followed suit. Kane observed that the lights were on. There was no answer.

"Something's happened," Kane hissed.

Davis tried the door. It was unlocked. The men rushed in.

"Becky! Donna!" Kane yelled.

Davis still had his gun drawn, as did both Watts and Walker. Kane didn't have a gun, but he ran into the living room. There were two glasses of juice sitting on the center table, hardly touched. Kane touched the velvet lining of the couch.

"Someone was sitting here."

"Actually, three people were sitting in this room, judging from the way the cushions are matted down," Davis said slowly.

Kane looked inside the side table drawer on a hunch. He looked up, quite disturbed. "Becky's gun is gone."

Watts was frowning. He looked out the window.

"Whatever happened here, the women were taken by surprise by someone. I think they've been taken away by this person."

Kane looked desperate. "We've got to ask the neighbors if

they saw anything."

Davis turned sharply, "Kane, where's your kids?"

"They're with Nadine, thank goodness. She'll have them till tomorrow."

At that moment, the phone rang. The ring startled everyone at first. Then Kane snatched it up.

"Kane residence."

"Kane? Let me speak to the chief," a male voice rang out. It had a hint of urgency to it.

"Who is this?"

"Let me speak to the damn chief. Now!"

Kane handed the cordless over to Davis.

"Hello. Davis here."

"Chief. Listen to me. You have to get over to the Broken Arrow rock quarry right away," a raspy voice said tensely.

"Who is this?"

"Never mind who this is. You need to get to the rock quarry right now. Go past the northern point, and park. Walk about three hundred yards into the woods. You'll find what you're looking for."

"What are you talking about? How did you know I was here? How do you know what I am looking for?"

"Are you going to ask questions all day or do your job, chief? Time's wasting!" the man was on edge.

"But what..."

The raspy stranger had hung up.

Davis hit the off button and swore. "Now what the hell is that all about?"

"You think it was Lemming?" Watts asked.

Davis nodded. "Didn't sound like Lemming. I have heard the voice before, though."

Kane nodded in agreement. "I don't think it was Lemming either."

Davis was lost in thought. Should they go to the rock quarry? If they did, and it was a wild goose chase, they might lose the track. On the other hand, this might be the lead they needed. He decided to play his hunch.

"Let's go. We need to go to the Broken Arrow rock quarry."

Watts frowned. "That's twenty five miles away. What's there?"

Davis opened the door. "Hopefully, exactly what we're looking for."

The four men headed north quickly. As they passed downtown, Davis got on his police radio and called for backup. He had the feeling that they may be needed. As he signed off, a look of dismay crossed his face.

"What's the matt..." Kane started to ask, and then saw what the problem was. They were slowing down. Traffic had stopped just ahead of them. It was a traffic jam.

"Damn!" Davis yelled and got on the police radio. "Breaker. This is Chief Chandler Davis. Someone tell me what this damn traffic's all about on the interstate near Welton Street."

Soon a voice cackled over the speaker. "Chief, there's a major traffic jam on the interstate going north."

Davis bellowed into his transmitter, "No shit you idiot! What's the problem?"

"Sorry chief. There's been a three-car pileup. Traffic's going to be backed up for hours."

Davis threw down his transmitter. "Son of a bitch!"

"Well, it looks like we're out of luck," Watts said.

"The hell we are," Davis said, swinging the car into the emergency lane. "Hold on."

He gunned the accelerator and sped past the stopped traffic, sirens blaring. The speedometer kept climbling.

Kane's knuckles went white from gripping his hand rest. "Uh chief, shouldn't we slow down? I mean, one of these cars might swing out in front of us."

"You want to find your wife?"

"Of course..."

"Then shut up."

A couple of miles up the road they slowed down. The accident was very gruesome. There were already ambulances and police there. The chief slowed down as a policeman flagged him down. He lowered his windshield to speak to the man.

"Need any help here? I have an urgent situation to go to."

The policeman was grim. "Go on ahead, chief. This is under control."

"Any fatalities? What happened?"

"Two fatalities. One was a seventeen year old. Looks like a DUI."

The chief shook his head. "Sorry to hear that. Well, we'd better go."

He raised his windshield back up and sped on ahead. The highway cleared of all cars, and he could now really turn on the speed. He turned his siren off but kept his blue lights on. He didn't tell the others, but he did not think that the outlook was very bright for the women. In his experience, very few kidnappers actually let their victims go. Most of them either killed them or were never heard from again. He did have some hope that the person who had called them would be of help somehow, since he had an idea of what was going on. He wished he knew what to expect himself.

"Chief, what exactly are we going to do once we get there?" Kane asked.

"You are going to stay in the car, while me and Walker go check out the tip."

Watts was angry. "I think I should go too, Chandler. I have a gun, and I can take care of myself."

"No way, you're not doing any such thing," Davis said, setting his jaw.

In about five minutes, he turned the car into an exit and veered to the right. Within two hundred yards, there was a sign on the side that read "Broken Arrow Rock Quarry". He turned into a dirt road that led up a hill. There were a lot of trees in this area. It was dark now, and the moon was almost full. The road wound around the hill and came to and end in front of an old house. It was obviously abandoned, but the rock quarry was plainly visible behind it. The chief put the car in park and radioed for backup. He and Detective Walker grabbed their flashlights and stepped out of the car. Watts also stepped out, and Davis motioned him back in.

Watts shook his head. "No way Chandler, I've been following this case for four years," he whispered.

Kane spoke up from inside the car. "I think I should go too. It's my wife that's missing."

Davis frowned. "Watts, you can come. Kane, you stay here. When backup comes, tell them where we are, if we're not back then."

Watts nodded, and the three men stepped forward. They

181

went around the building and stared at the rock quarry. The woods began almost right behind the quarry. This was where the anonymous caller had told them to go.

"Into the woods," Davis said, his gun drawn. Walker already had his gun out, and so did Watts. They were going into a situation where they did not know what to expect. Davis half expected to be fired at any second. His years of experience gave him the feeling that this was indeed a very dangerous situation.

They walked about a hundred yards and came onto a clearing. Davis stopped walking and looked around. The moonlight shone clearly through the crack in the trees. There was nothing to be seen except lightning bugs and the dark shadows of trees all around them. He turned off his flashlight. Walker kept his on.

"So? What now?" Watts asked, a little perplexed. He had expected something to have happened already.

"I don't know," Davis said, studying his surroundings. There wasn't much to see. The clearing was full of tall brush and bushes. A small mound of dirt the shape of a pitcher's mound was to his left. Beyond that lay more trees.

"Let's go on ahead," Walker said.

"Wait!" Davis said, studying a bush to his right. He had noticed something.

"Really," Watts echoed, "Where are we going to go? There's nothing but forest and trees and..."

"Be quiet!" Davis hissed, edging his way forward toward the bush. He pointed his gun at it. Quickly he flicked on his flashlight and shone it on the bush.

"Come on out of there!"

Nothing happened.

"I said, come on out from behind the bush, Lemming. I can see you, and I have a gun pointed right at you."

A figure rose from behind the bush. The light from the flashlight shone directly on his face. It was indeed the celebrated P.I. He was smiling.

"What's going on, chief?" he asked innocently.

Davis held his gun steady. "You tell me."

Lemming threw his arms up. "Just out getting some fresh air," he said, coming out from behind the bush.

"Stay where you are," Davis said sharply.

Lemming was still smiling. "Oh now chief, you're not going to play the ugly policeman, are you?"

"Throw down any weapons you have in front of you," Davis ordered.

"Okay, but please take that light off my face. I can't see a thing."

Davis obliged, and immediately regretted his action. With the speed of a cobra, Lemming had produced a gun fron his jacket pocket. He had it pointed at him before he could move.

"Drop that gun!" Walker yelled, his gun fixed on Lemming. Watts also had his Beretta aimed at the detective's head.

Davis's finger quivered on the trigger. "Drop the gun, Lemming. It's over. You're outnumbered three to one. Even if you shot onc of us, you'd be dead. There is no escape."

Lemming was calm. He kept his gun on Davis. "You're right, chief. There is one problem, though. If you kill me, you'll never find out where the three women are. That is why you're here, isn't it?"

Davis set his jaw. A trickle of sweat fell on his face. Lemming had a point, but he could not let him have the upper hand.

Lemming continued, "I think you three better throw down your guns, chief. That is, if you want to know where the women are."

"How do we know that you haven't killed them already?"

"You don't. You'd better make up your mind, though. They don't have much time."

Davis was the picture of intensity. "We can't throw down our guns, Lemming. You'd kill us all."

Lemming smiled wickedly, keeping his gun trained on Davis's head. "My, you must think me a monster, chief! Of course I could do that, but can you risk the lives of three women like that? You're the good guy here."

Davis shook his head. "We can't throw down our guns. You have no intention of letting those women go."

From his shirt pocket, Lemming got a cigarette with his left hand. He lit it and blew a cloud of smoke into the clear air. Not once did his eyes leave the three men. Davis's grip on his gun tightened.

"I see," he said quietly. "Then what do we do, gentlemen? It appears we have a stalemate."

"Lemming, listen to me," Davis said, "You can still make the right decision. Give up now, and we'll try and work a deal with the courts. If you don't, then you're putting yourself in deeper and deeper."

Lemming laughed. "Chief, you really don't think I'm a fool, do you? I am pretty sure you know now that I killed two girls, one woman, and a dumb hitman. What kind of deal do you hope to work for me, huh? A choice between lethal injection or the chair? No thanks chief. You and I both know that this is going down one of two ways. Me in a body bag, or you three in a body bag. I prefer the latter, but I guess the odds are against me."

"Let me take him out, chief," Walker said grimly, "He'll go down before he can get off a shot."

"Shut up!" Davis yelled, "Listen to me, Lemming. It doesn't have to be that way. You've killed some people, don't kill more, and don't get yourself killed. You have a good reputation in Denver. I don't know why you did all this, but I know there's reasons for everything we do. Now put your gun down and do the right thing."

"Sorry chief. Can't do that. I guess I'm going to have to start the shooting. I may be able to get all three of you before you hit me. It is dark, after all."

He cocked his gun. There was a disturbance behind him and the sound of feet. He turned around to see a figure bearing down on him. His gun went off, followed by a scream. The figure fell and crashed into Lemming, knocking him down. Davis leaped forward, trying to isolate the fallen P.I. Unfortunately, Lemming had not been knocked down very hard, and he sprang up, the gun still in his hands. Davis stopped in his tracks, as the gun was pointed at him again. Watts and Walker, who had lost sight of what was happening, had frozen.

"Stop right there chief. Do not cock your gun at me."

Davis swore under his breath. His gun was still in his hand, but he did not have it raised. Lemming had the advantage now.

"You two, frick and frack, drop your guns unless you want the chief's brains blown away. Right now!" Lemming had suddenly turned very businesslike.

Watts and Walker dropped their guns.

"No! You dumb-asses!" Davis swore.

Lemming picked up the chief's flashlight, which had fallen. He shone it on the strange figure that had attacked him seconds earlier. The man was lying on the grass, moaning. He seemed to have a bullet wound in his shoulder.

"Well, look here. It's Mark Kane. The gang's all here!"

Mark Kane stared at Lemming and tried to get up. A spasm of pain shot through his left shoulder and he crumpled back down.

"You son of a bitch!" he said, gritting his teeth.

Lemming shook his finger at Kane. "Now, now, Kane. Insulting my mother will do you no good. You've been a royal pain through this whole damn ordeal. It'll be a pleasure to finally get rid of you."

Kane sat up. "Get rid of me? Who are you going to frame that one on, you piece of shit?"

Lemming motioned to the three men in front of him. "You three get over here with Mr. shoulder wound here and keep him company. I want to be able to keep an eye on all of you without him thinking he's a football player again."

Davis, Walker and Watts walked over to where Kane sat. Davis bent down to inspect Kane's wound. The bullet had gone right through the shoulder. He took off his jacket and pressed down on the wound, which was now flowing with blood.

"We need to get him to a hospital," he said, turning to Lemming. "He's losing a lot of blood."

Lemming's smile was back. "He shouldn't have tried to be a hero. Anyway, it won't do him much good anyway. I'm afraid I'm going to have to kill all of you now. So sad, so sad."

Davis held up his hands. "Don't be crazy, Lemming. Killing all of us won't set you free, they'll hunt you down."

"Really? Who will?"

"I've already radioed for backup."

Lemming laughed. "You're behind a big mountain, chief. Are you sure your message got through?"

Kane spoke up. "Just tell me one thing. Why? Why did you do all this? And why did you frame me for it? And where are the women?"

Lemming shook his head gravely. "Sorry buddy. Like I said

to those women, I'm taking that one to my grave. As for the women, I guess they literally will do the same."

Kane's face was a thunderstorm. "Tell me what you did with them, you little..."

"Enough! It's time to end this little show," Lemming said, lifting his gun. He pointed it at Kane.

"No!" Davis yelled and closed his eyes as the loud noise of a gun went off in his head. There was a loud scream, and someone fell. He opened his eyes.

Lemming was lying on the ground, writhing in pain. His cigarette had fallen from his mouth. His reflexes took over. Bending over, he picked up the gun that lay by the wounded David Lemming. Walker also picked up his gun and rushed over to the fallen detective. Watts stood by, transfixed. Kane looked around wildly. "All right asshole!" Walker screamed, pointing his gun at Lemming," Put your hands behind you right now!"

Davis motioned to him. He turned over the body of Lemming, which had now gone limp. He checked for a pulse underneath his arm. It was faint.

"Walker, go down to the car and radio for an ambulance, now!"

Walker ran off, with Watts on his heels.

Davis looked into the face of David Lemming. He picked up the cigarette from the ground and threw it at his face. "These things are really bad for you, you prick."

"Chief, look!" Kane spoke up.

A figure was walking up to them from the woods. He had a rifle on his shoulder. On reflex, Davis went for his gun and pointed it at the figure.

"Don't move! Stop where you are!"

The figure stopped and raised his hand. "Don't shoot chief. You've been looking for me," a raspy voice called out.

Davis grabbed his flashlight and shone it on the figure. It illuminated the face clearly. The light shone on the face of a tired looking Robert Blackwood.

"You!" Davis exclaimed, lowering his gun.

Blackwood walked forward and put his rifle down. "Yes, it's me. No need to thank me for saving your life."

Davis was hesitant. "I'm not sure what to do with you.

Where did you spring from?"

"Listen chief, we can stand here and waste time, but I think you have a much more pressing problem," Blackwood was irritated.

"My only problem right now is the women that are still missing, and unless you know..."

Blackwood held up his hands. He started to look around in the darkness for something. "Chief, let me borrow your flashlight."

Davis threw the long flashlight over to the muscular man. He looked very grim. Flicking on the light, he shone it around. His gaze fell on the pitching mound-like hill some twenty yards away. He raced over to the mound, and looked down at it. He bent over and picked up something. It was an empty box of large trash bags.

"He was digging here," he muttered, and looked up. "Chief, do we have any shovels?"

"Shovels? What do you need with..."

"Chief, we don't have time! We have to dig, now!" Blackwood was starting to get panicky.

Davis ran over to the spot where Blackwood was standing and looked at the ground. It looked like it was freshly tossed, as if someone had recently piled dirt there. His face turned white.

"Oh my God."

Kane's bleeding was starting to subside, but he felt weak. Keeping his jacket tourniquet on, he hobbled over to the spot.

"What are you saying? Why do we need to dig?"

Blackwood didn't answer. He was starting to look around again.

Davis spoke up. "Listen Blackwood, we caught Lemming up here hiding. I don't think he had time to go down to his car, wherever it is. Therefore..."

"...Therefore his shovels are still here!" Blackwood finished. "Quickly, look!"

Kane was still thunderstruck. "You're not saying what I think you're saying."

At that moment, Watts and Walker came running back up. Seeing the three men searching the grounds, they ran toward them. Watts tripped over something and fell flat on his face.

"Damn! Who left a damn shovel out here in the middle of nowhere?"

To his surprise, he saw Davis and Blackwood come running to his aid. However, they didn't help him up, but leaped on the shovel, still jutting out from the ground.

"Hurry!" Davis cried, and the two men ran back to where they were.

He hastily got up, brushed himself off, and ran over to the mound of dirt the rest of the men were on. Blackwood was furiously digging away.

"Walker, do we have any shovels in the squad cars?" Davis asked frantically.

"Well yes, we keep one in each car for the snow."

"Get it, now!"

Perplexed, Walker ran back down to the car. Within three minutes, they were digging with two shovels. The men took turn so as they wouldn't slow down. In about thirty minutes, Blackwood's shovel revealed a black plastic-like substance.

"It's a garbage bag! Dig it out!" he screamed.

Within two minutes, the large bag was dug out. There appeared to be something large in it. There was another bag underneath it, and it was dug out quickly. The men dragged the two bags out of the hole that they had dug in frantic pace. There was another bag on the bottom, and it was also dragged out. By the time the last bag was dragged out, Davis and Watts had opened the first two bags and dragged out two bodies. They were Rebecca Kane and Donna Houseman. The third bag held a woman that they had never seen, but they assumed that this was the elusive Joyce Lemming.

Kane knelt down and felt the pulses of the three women. Becky Kane and Donna Houseman had very faint pulses, but Joyce Lemming did not. He immediately started CPR on his wife and Donna, in turn. Davis stood by impatiently. Walker tried to revive the cold body of Joyce Lemming.

"This is not good," Davis gasped, "Where are those damn ambulances!"

"I wonder how long they've been down there," Blackwood said, his face wearing a frown.

"I'd say probably a couple of hours," Watts said, still trying to revive the limp wife of David lemming, "It's a good thing he wrapped them in bags, they had a little air to breathe for a short time."

Becky Kane suddenly started to choke and gasp to life. Her husband leaped up.

"She's coming out of it!"

Blackwood assisted Kane in steadying her, as she did indeed seem to be breathing more normally now. Her eyelids fluttered open and she stared into the face of her husband vacantly. At that moment they heard the sound of approaching ambulances. Suddenly the din of a helicopter filled the air, and as the men looked up, they saw a Lifestar helicopter from city general. Kane breathed a sigh of relief.

"About time, too!"

Soon, doctors and paramedics filled the scene and took over the situation. The place was suddenly filled with people as cars and vans filled with local media rushed into the scene. Kane recognized one of the reporters, as she worked with his wife. The situation was somewhat more stable, although the three women were not out of the woods. Davis sat down on a tree stump. He was tired. Kane sat down next to him.

"Tough day chief?"

Davis laughed through his nose. "You know Kane, the older I get, the more bizarre the criminals get."

Kane stared at the helicopter as it flew away with the three women and David Lemming securely inside it. "I guess I'd better go to the hospital. You think they'll be okay?"

Davis shook his head. "They'll make it. I have a gut feeling."

"Where did Blackwood get himself lost at?"

Davis turned to face Kane. "If it wasn't for him, we'd have lost those three women tonight."

"No chief, if it wasn't for him, the ambulances would have been picking up six dead bodies tonight."

Chief Davis looked up at the moon. He really needed to get some sleep.

☠

Conclusion

The next day was a nice day. The sun was shining brightly in the Denver sky as a squad car pulled up to the Kane house. Mark Kane, still with the taste of bacon in his mouth, opened the door before the two men could knock. Chief Davis and Donald Watts walked in, smiling. Kane could finally allow them in without feeling a sense of dread.

"Morning Mark, have a good night's sleep?" Davis asked, wiping his feet.

"Best sleep I've had in two weeks!" Kane said, grinning. "Have a seat gentlemen."

Rebecca Kane came into the room. She smiled at the visitors. "Come on in, we figured you'd be here soon."

Davis beamed. "I guess they let you out last night?"

Becky Kane smiled. "Yeah, I wasn't so bad. Donna got out this morning, and so did Joyce. It could have been much worse."

The two men sat down, as Kane went into the kitchen to pour himself a glass of milk. "You fellows eat breakfast yet? How about some eggs?"

"No thanks, Mark. We're just here to fill you in. Lemming talked this morning," Davis said.

Kane came back into the living room and sat down, sipping his milk. "So he's okay? I thought he may die."

"No, he wasn't as badly hurt as we thought at first. The bullet didn't hit anything vital, which is probably unlucky for him. He's facing some serious charges."

Becky Kane sat down beside her husband. "So he confessed?"

Watts beamed. "Better. He even told us why he did it. The man looked defeated this morning."

"I guess I'll begin this story," Davis said. "It all started in 1989, when David Lemming met a young student named Virginia Kelly on one of his cases. He fell for her immediately, but

190

unfortunately, he was married. He started an affair with her, not telling her that he was married. This went on for a little while. Once, Scott Kelly even walked in on the two. Things started to go wrong when one day Virginia found out about the marriage. What she did is follow Lemming back to his house, because she was suspicious as to why they never went back to his place. When she found out about his marriage, she gave him an ultimatum. He had to leave his wife for her, or she would expose him. Strangely, Lemming didn't want to leave his wife, so he offered her money to keep quiet. Kelly agreed to this, as this would help her with her drugs, and she was desperate to find a source for her drug money. This was the perfect solution. For a while, the payments came her way, and Lemming got to keep his secret. Lemming realized that his money was going down the drain, and decided to do something. He went up to Virginia Kelly's apartment one night when he knew her roommates would not be there. She let him in, thinking that he had money. He knocked her over the head and stuck a knife in her throat. He then hurriedly left, not knowing that someone had seen him leave. This someone had seen him before, and knew who he was, due to his reputation in the city..."

"Traci McKinley!" Kane interjected.

"Right," Davis said, "Anyway, Lemming came back a little later and pretended to be investigating. He ran into a man who identified himself as John Kirby. This was actually Robert Blackwood, who was seeing Miss Kelly at the time. Blackwood was on his way to see her, and to his shock, she had been murdered. Lemming chased Blackwood away, but the name John Kirby stuck to his subconscious. The nest day, Lemming interviewed Traci McKinley, and she hinted to him that she may have seen something. He gave her a card to call him. She did, and told him that she had seen the whole thing. A man named Michael Barnard was hastily framed by Lemming, but he didn't plan it well, and it didn't hold up in court."

"I can vouch for that," Watts said dejectedly.

"Traci McKinley started the nightmare all over for Lemming," Davis continued, "She demanded money for her silence. She even put two and two together and figured out why he murdered Virginia Kelly. Lemming had to protect his reputation and marriage, so he kept paying, explaining to his wife that the

191

reason for their money problems was a lack of good cases. He didn't want to resort to another murder. He felt that leaving well enough alone was good. He was sure that Traci would stop asking for money soon enough. She didn't. This went on for four years. Finally, Lemming reached the end of his rope with McKinley. He devised a way to get rid of her. He hired a hit man to do the job. The hit man bungled the job, and got cold feet. It turned out that he wasn't that good a hitman at all. Lemming did have a back up plan already in motion. He had come up with a plan to kill her himself. This plan had to be better than the first one, which was not planned well at all. He went to the airport and went straight to the bar. The first person to come in would get his glass stolen, and be framed for the murder that was going to take place."

"And I'm the idiot who had to go into the bar," Kane said disgustedly.

Davis smiled. "Yes you were. Anyway, he had to set it up. He called you, set up a bogus lunch for the time he was going to commit the murder, and then went about it. He went to Traci McKinley's house, killed her, and walked out. As he walked out, he saw Teresa Brown staring at him. He decided to protect his ass and threatened her. She was scared, so she listened. He gave her some money, and convinced her to state that bogus story about seeing Kane at the murder site. He figured that would be enough to convict him."

Watts broke in. "But things didn't go well. Travis Singleton, the hit man, was being a pain. He decided to bump him off as well. Meanwhile, the chief was not sold on Kane's guilt, and he was on to Teresa Brown lying. She was on the verge of cracking. He couldn't let that happen, so he set up the meeting with Kane to go talk to the Brown woman. He shows up early, kills the woman, and leaves, waiting for Kane to show up. When he does, he comes in behind him, and acts like he's shocked to see Kane there. That should convince the chief that Kane is guilty, for who would murder Teresa Brown but the person who she can identify in court? And here's a celebrated private detective to vouch for the fact that he saw Kane there. One thing goes wrong, though. Kane, you panic, hit him over the head, and disappear. He hadn't figured on this, but realizes that he can use it to his advantage. He gets out of the hospital, and watches your house, hoping you'd lead him to

Kane. Sure enough, he spots Donna and Rebecca leave together. He follows them to the airport, and actually gets on the same plane to Atlanta with them. He's having a worrying thought though. Suppose Kane had figured it out and that's why he had hit him over the head? When he follows the women out to the lake, he thinks that they have had a conversation with Kane. He decides to lock them in the barn, and throws their car into the lake. In the morning, he comes back to set the barn on fire. Kane spots it and saves them. Lemming, now thoroughly pissed, returns to Denver right behind Kane. Things are snowballing, in his mind. He gets paranoid and thinks that Kane, his wife, and Donna are plotting to get some evidence on him. He decides that he must get rid of the women somehow, so he seizes his chance when we are all in the police department. He rushes out to Kane's house, where as luck would have it, he finds the women. He hadn't counted on his wife being there, but now he has to get rid of her too. He loads them into his car and comes up with a devious plan. He's going to bury them alive out at the rock quarry, where no one ever goes. Then he would take the women's jewelry, along with some ashes, and roll the car down a mountain. People would think that they burned up in an accident. No remains of a body would be found, and it would go away."

"Fortunately for us, someone was on to him," Davis broke in, "Robert Blackwood had decided that things weren't looking good for him, but he knew that he was innocent, therefore he had to find the killer. He decided to watch the house of the person who he thought was the killer."

"Who was that?" Kane asked.

Davis chuckled. "He thought it was you, Mrs. Kane."

Rebecca Kane was stunned. "Me!"

"Yes, Blackwood confessed this morning that he thought it was you who had done the whole thing out of jealousy. Don't ask me jealousy of what, I don't think he even knew. Anyway, he was watching this house at the time Lemming drove up and sneaked into your house through a back window. He even saw him swipe your gun, Mrs. Kane, which was in a kitchen drawer. You see, he was watching the rear of your house. His suspicions about Lemming were aroused, and confirmed in a few minutes when he came out of the house and forced the women in his car, hands bound and mouths gagged. He decided to follow Lemming, and followed him all the way out to the quarry."

"I think Joyce and Donna saw him when we were tied to a tree," Becky Kane said, "They were trying to get my attention, but I couldn't understand them."

"Right," Davis said, "Now Blackwood observes Lemming dig his little burial plot, and he starts to suspect what is going on. He gets in his car and comes back to this house to see if we're there. Sure enough, we were. He gets on his cell phone and calls me, telling me to get my ass over to the rock quarry, all the while not daring to show his face for fear of being arrested. When we leave, he comes along behind us. He has his rifle in his car, and gets it out. He comes to the clearing and notices what is going on. He has to act fast. Quickly he sets up, and shoots Lemming just in time. You guys know the rest."

"Why didn't he just pull his rifle on Lemming when he was digging his hole?" Mark Kane asked.

"I wish he would have," Davis said, "But he was afraid that if it came down to gunplay and he killed him, he would get arrested. He wanted us to find you, for selfish reasons. I guess we all have to look out for number one."

"Well my God, I would vouch for him and say that it was Lemming!" Rebecca Kane said adamantly.

"Let's not criticize and browbeat his thinking too much," Watts put in, "If it weren't for him, we'd all be dead. We really owe him a debt of gratitude."

"Yes, don't forget that the real monster here was Lemming," Davis pointed out.

"Yes, Lemming. What a psycho he is," Rebecca observed sadly.

"Not a psycho," Davis said introspectively, "Just a guy whose whole world crashed around him."

"I guess you could say that things just got way out of control for him," Mark Kane said sadly.

Davis was surprised. "You sound like you feel for him. After all he did to you and your family? He almost sent you jail, almost killed you and your wife, and made your life living hell."

Kane shook his head. "Don't get me wrong, chief. I don't feel for him. What he's done will haunt us forever. What I am saying is that in some weird way, I understand his increasing paranoia and feeling of helplessness. I was in the same boat, for different reasons."

Becky spoke up. "What will happen to him, you think?"

"I'm prosecuting him," Watts said, a crooked smile on his face. "I'm going to throw the book at him. If he's lucky he'll get the death penalty. A guy like him who has put away so many criminals doesn't want to end up in jail, believe me."

Davis got up. "We'd better be going. I hope your family gets back its peace, Mark."

Kane got up and shook his hand. "That's the first time you called me by my first name, chief. It's kind of nice."

"Good day to you two," Watts said, "I'll see you two at the trial."

The two men left. Kane shut the door behind them and looked at his wife, who was smiling at him. It was nice to take this day off. As the sun shone through the window, he sat down on the couch beside her. She didn't say anything, but put her arms around him. Completely relaxed, he stared out the front window and saw the neighbor's dog urinating on his lawn. For once, it did not bother him. He smiled, sat back, and flicked on the television.

☠☠

Printed in the United States
20147LVS00001BA/9